Murder With a Splash of Vanilla

Kristy T Dixon

To Shelly Szymanski, April Watson, and Cindy Price

Chapter 1

"Ivy Elon Clark! Get off there. You're gonna fall on your head."

I balanced myself on two bricks, fifteen feet up on the front of my diner. The bricks were uneven and jutted out. I had my free hand on another unruly brick, and I wasn't feeling good about my life's choices. It had seemed like a good place to stand when I'd stepped off my ladder to reach the last strand of Christmas lights. Now I wasn't sure I could find the ladder again with my foot.

If I fell, I would try to fall to the left and land on the big white-and-red awning just below me and to the side. It wouldn't save me from dropping the rest of the way to the ground, but it was possible I'd fall into the snow pile next to the sidewalk.

"I'm not joking, Ivy," Sheriff Jett Malone said from somewhere below me. "That doesn't look safe at all."

My fingers burned, and I dropped the lights and grabbed another brick. I could fall and die, or swallow my pride and admit my predicament. "I can't move," I said, "and I'm going to slip."

I heard the metal ladder creak as Jett climbed the rickety steps. I closed my eyes, sure I couldn't hold on any longer.

"I'm going to tell you where to put your foot so you can put it on the top of the ladder, alright?" Jett said.

"Mm-hmm," I muttered. I was glad I'd come up without my coat because I was beginning to sweat.

"It's right below your foot. Lower it slowly."

I shifted slightly and felt like I might fall. "I can't. If I take my foot off, I'll lose my grip."

I heard Jett sigh, then more metal creaking from the ladder. Jett's hands went around my waist. "Now put your foot down. Be careful, or we'll both fall."

Now that he was holding up a lot of my weight, I could move my foot down and find the top of the ladder. I moved my other foot but kept my hands on the bricks.

"I'm going to go down a step," Jett said. "Let go and step down with me."

I took a step, careful not to land on him. I was already embarrassed enough. It was slow going, but I finally reached the shoveled sidewalk. My heart was pounding, and my hands were sweaty.

"What do you think you were doing?" Jett asked, his hands on his hips.

I took a deep, shaky breath. "I got a letter from the town. It said if I didn't take my Christmas lights down by the end of January, I would get fined."

"And that was the best way to do it?"

"Probably not."

"What would have happened if I hadn't come by?"

I grinned. "I would have fallen on the awning and rolled off into a pile of snow."

He shook his head and didn't smile. "Why didn't you have the people working on your expansion help you? They have better ladders."

"I didn't want to bug them. Besides, they would probably charge me more." The diner expansion was going faster than I expected, and I didn't want to distract the workers.

"Better to pay them than the hospital." He opened the door to the diner and held it while I walked in. He put a hand on my back and guided me to the kitchen. I didn't protest and draw attention. When we entered, José and Anton looked up from where they were cooking.

"Uh-oh," José said. "Ivy looks guilty, and Jett looks annoyed. Did Ivy stumble across a dead body?"

I grinned. "Not today."

"She was standing on bricks sticking out of the diner while trying to take down Christmas lights."

José shook his head. "Come on, Ivy. You know better than that."

I rolled my eyes. "It was fine."

"You couldn't get down," Jett pointed out, running a hand through his brown hair.

"I would've figured it out."

"Let me see your hands," Jett said.

I smiled and held them behind my back. I hadn't looked at them, but they hurt, so I was sure they were scratched up.

"Next time, ask me," José said. "I have a better ladder. That one you use is awful."

"I'll get a new one someday. I just don't think about it unless I need it." My mouth turned down, and I glared at Jett. "How did you know my middle name?"

For the first time since I'd seen him today, he smiled. "That's my secret."

"You better not use it again."

"Why? What's wrong with it?"

José glanced up. "What is it?"

"It doesn't matter," I said.

Jett grinned. "I don't know why you care. It's not bad."

"Not if you're a rich business owner and a man. I used to like it until he got popular. Now when people find out, they ask me if I can get them a deal on a Tesla."

Anton laughed. "It's not Elon?"

I sighed.

"It is?" José asked. "That's awesome. I knew a girl named Elon once. It's not only a guy's name."

I shook my head. "I never said it was."

Jett's phone buzzed, and he pulled it from his pocket. His smile fell. "My deputy needs me. I'm starting to wonder who's the boss in this town."

"Don't let Leford boss you around," I said. "We can't have that man running the town."

"That's for sure," Anton muttered. "That guy is a leech."

I went to the mixer and plugged it in. Tonight was book club at the diner, and those ladies could consume a lot of cookies. I grabbed the ugly cat apron Jett had given me and pulled it over my head. I couldn't ever let him know how hideous the neon material was.

"When I come back for dinner, I don't want to see Ivy hanging from anything. Got it?" Jett said.

"Sure," José assured him. "We'll keep an eye on her."

I just smiled. Jett stood next to me with his arms crossed. I looked up at him.

"I'm not kidding, Ivy. That was dangerous. Don't do it again."

I swallowed and turned away when I realized I was staring at his mouth. Sometimes I wonder about myself. I couldn't imagine many women looking at handsome Sheriff Jett Malone and not feeling a little lightheaded.

"I won't, don't worry. I have a lot to keep me busy."

"Good." He winked. "Save me some cookies. Those book club ladies are stingy about their desserts. It's hard to get them to share."

"I will." I watched him walk out of the kitchen and kept staring through the serving window as he left.

"You could take a picture of him and hang it on the wall," Anton teased. "Then you could look at it whenever you want."

I glared at him. "I think you've been hanging around José and Boyd too much."

He laughed. "Probably."

"Anton has a date," José said.

"Really?" I asked.

Anton frowned and pulled off his hairnet. He rubbed a hand through his black hair. "Why is everyone acting like it's some kind of miracle? Under this horrible hairnet is a man with attractive hair and a killer personality."

"We aren't doubting that," I said. "It's just that there aren't a lot of women around here under thirty."

"I met her online. She lives close to Wichita."

"Have you done online dating before?" I asked. It wasn't something I would ever want to try. It felt awkward. Not that meeting people in other circumstances wasn't, but people could say anything on dating profiles.

"No. I've talked to some people, but this is my first time meeting someone."

"Well, good for you. I hope you have fun."

"I need something to do now that the holidays are over."

I grabbed some butter and began peeling off the wrapper. "I've survived my first holiday season in Muddy Creek. Now I feel like we need something exciting. January is always so dull."

José looked thoughtful. "You haven't solved a murder in a while."

"January's too boring for a murder," Anton said.

"I don't think Muddy Creek can survive another one," I said. Since I'd moved here, there had been three, and I solved all of them with the help of José, Boyd, and Jett. We weren't the obvious choice for something like this, but we made it work.

The kitchen door opened, and Boyd came in. "Hey, all. Do you guys notice anything different about me?"

I placed the butter in the mixing bowl and studied Boyd. I had no idea what could be different. He was sucking in his stomach, but that couldn't be what he meant.

"Your clothes match?" Anton asked.

"Nope. I mean, they might, but that's not it."

"You whitened your teeth?" José guessed.

"It's my hair!" Boyd declared.

I raised my eyebrow. He was bald. He'd been bald since I met him.

Anton grinned. "I hate to tell you this, Boyd, but you don't have hair."

"But now I shaved off the little bit I did have. Next, I'm growing a goatee. It's the thing to do when you go bald. I read about it in a magazine when I was at the dentist. Barbra will have to be impressed."

I smiled, and José chuckled.

That reminded me. I needed to go to Barbra's house to finish helping her clean it out. Barbra hasn't thrown anything away in the past thirty years, and I'm helping her declutter. I wasn't going to make it today, but maybe tomorrow.

"What do you think about facial hair, Ivy?" Boyd asked.

My mouth turned down. I didn't want to kill Boyd's enthusiasm. "It's not my favorite."

"Not at all?"

"Well, I like it when it's just stubble and between days two and five of not shaving."

The room burst into laughter.

"That's pretty specific," José said.

Boyd arched his eyebrow. "And it sounds like a certain sheriff we know."

I felt heat run across my neck. I couldn't believe I admitted that, especially to these guys. I went to the large pantry and grabbed the brown sugar.

"How long are you gonna wear that ugly apron, Ivy?" Boyd asked. "I think you've worn it enough to trick Jett into thinking you like it."

"It's fine," I lied, measuring the sugar.

"If you like neon green, I guess. Don't listen to me. Once you hit seventy, you can't be trusted to give fashion advice."

I just smiled. Boyd was like the grandpa I never had, and I didn't know how I made it most of my life without him.

José's phone rang, and he glanced at it. "Hey, Anton? Watch my pot. I need to take this." He stepped out the back door of the diner, and I shivered when the cool air blew in.

"Are you short-staffed tonight?" Boyd asked.

"Not too bad. It's not busy when it's this cold. I miss Livy. She texted me that she's enjoying college."

José's mouth turned up. "All two weeks of it?"

Livy had been a server here, and I missed her. She'd been consistent, and people liked her.

"You know you had a ladder sitting out front? It was blocking part of the doorway," said Boyd.

"Oh, I forgot. I'll get it in a minute."

"It's not there anymore. I saw Jett take it."

"Did he put it away?"

"I doubt it. He walked off toward the sheriff's office with it."

I sighed. Now I would have to report a stolen ladder to the person who stole it.

Anton laughed. "Jett knows if you don't have a ladder, you can't get into as much trouble."

Boyd sat on a stool. "You and Jett have the strangest relationship. When are the two of you going to stop messing around and get to some sparking?"

Anton dumped seasoning onto a burger. "That's the question on the lips of every citizen of Muddy Creek... at least if sparking means what I think it does. Dating or is it just kissing? I imagine two people sitting on a porch swing cuddling like in an old movie."

"That's it," Boyd said with a laugh.

I shook my head. "You two are ridiculous. We're friends, just like I'm friends with you guys."

Anton chuckled. "I've never seen you watch Boyd until he was out of sight."

Boyd's eyes sparkled. "That's for sure. We aren't blind around here, girlie."

I shook my head and went to the fridge for some eggs. The teasing wouldn't be so bad if I didn't have an enormous crush on Jett. I kept it to myself, but everyone seemed to enjoy shipping the two of us together.

"Have you ever gone on a date with him?" Anton asked.

"No."

Boyd smirked. "Not unless you count stakeouts and car chases. I think those should count. If they do, you've been on tons of dates."

"I've done more of that stuff with you than Jett," I protested.

José came into the kitchen with a huge smile on his face. "Guess who that was?"

I shrugged.

"Silvia Clements."

The name sounded familiar, but I couldn't place it.

"Come on. Silvia Clements? Her father was Zeb Clements."

"Oh! The people Barbra got her enormous wardrobe from." Barbra had gotten a wardrobe from an estate sale. We planned on going through it to see if anything was interesting, but things kept coming up.

"The Clementses have a huge Christmas party every year. They missed it this year because they were sick, so they're doing it next week. They want us to cater it."

My eyes lit up. "That's huge!"

"She said she's heard a lot of good things since you took over."

"It's going to have to be perfect. From what I've heard, the Clementses don't mingle with people from town."

José nodded. "I've never seen any of them. They're kind of snobbish. Even on the phone, she sounded condescending. Still, they're rich and influential."

This was exciting and scary. We had to get this done right. With luck, it would lead to even more catering jobs. It's something we hadn't done but had talked about.

"I'll leave it all to you," I told José.

He grinned. "It's going to be perfect."

Chapter 2

"Are you ready?" Barbra asked me. She stood in front of Zeb Clements's oak wardrobe and touched the handle.

I clasped my hands together and forced myself not to bounce up and down. I'd been wondering what was inside for months. "Do it!"

Barbra pushed her purple hair behind her ear and grinned. She grabbed the handle and pulled it open.

I stared in and frowned. "Great. It looks like you bought all of Zeb Clements's clothing. I guess I shouldn't be surprised. It is a wardrobe, after all."

Barbra laughed. "It looks like there are some things at the bottom. I can't kneel. My knees aren't what they used to be."

I crouched and pulled out a pair of dress shoes. They looked like they'd never been worn. I pulled out another pair that looked almost exactly the same.

Barbra shook her head when I pulled out the fifth pair. "Rich people have some funny habits." I didn't say anything, but I'd already thrown away or donated about twenty pairs of shoes that Barbra had stowed away. She was the biggest pack rat I'd ever seen.

I held up another pair. "Maybe we can sell it all online. They're high-end brands. We can call them eccentric millionaire's shoes."

"It's worth a try."

I pulled everything out of the bottom, finding nothing exciting. "There has to be something good in here," I said, running my hand over the wooden bottom. My fingers ran across a handle in the back. "Aha!" I pulled on the handle, and a false bottom opened.

"What is it?" Barbra asked, peering over my shoulder.

"Just some papers," I said, pulling them out. I looked down, and my eyes widened. "It says The Last Will and Testament of Zeb Clements."

"What does the sticky note say?"

I looked down at the blue note on the will and squinted to read the small writing. "This is a copy of my true will. I don't trust the original to go unaltered."

"Sounds like a mystery," Barbra said. "They sure seem to find you. I'm surprised there's not a body."

"It's only a mystery if someone altered the original will. I don't think there's a way for us to know without asking to see it, and no one's going to show us."

"Let me see," Barbra said, holding out her hand. I gave it to her, and she scanned it. "Not too exciting. He left an equal portion of all his money to his two children and three grandchildren. I'll put this in an envelope and mail it to the Clements's mansion."

I nodded and pulled out my phone. "Let me take a picture of it first." I focused my phone and took two pictures. I wasn't sure why, but it might be useful someday. "I hope you didn't pay too much for all this stuff. You can probably make a profit, but it's nothing exciting."

"That's alright. It was fun. I've appreciated your help to declutter. Even though we still have a lot to do, I feel better about my house."

I smiled. "I'm happy to help. I've enjoyed your company."

Barbra grinned. "You get a lot of company at the diner. Sometimes I think I should live right in the middle of town. They should build some retirement homes since the population is getting older. It would be nice not to have to drive at my age."

"Have you ever thought about remarrying?"

She laughed. "At my age? That's crazy. I don't have the time or energy to date, and where will I find someone who will put up with me?"

"I bet Boyd would put up with you," I teased.

She took a deep breath through her nose and gave me a pointed look. "Let's not get into that."

"You spend a lot of time together. You could both sell your houses and move to the middle of town."

Barbra sat on the armrest of the couch. "I'll admit, I've thought about it once or twice. Boyd's a good guy, and I enjoy spending time with him. I'm just set in my ways."

"Boyd seems adaptable."

She laughed again. "I think he is. Still, I don't know if I have the kind of energy it would take to keep him in line. He's always getting into some kind of trouble, and the man isn't young!"

"You get around well. What if you live twenty to thirty more years? Do you want to be alone?"

Barbra raised her eyebrow. "You might live seventy more years. Are you going to spend them alone?"

I forced a smile. "I have Creepers."

"And cats live how long?"

"Hopefully forever." It was hard to believe I'd spent so much of my life without Creepers. He made everything more entertaining.

"I know a handsome sheriff who is available."

"He's too young for you," I said, picking up my purse.

Barbra roared with laughter. "That's for dang sure. He's not going to stay available forever."

"I have to go," I said. "I hope you'll dream about Boyd."

Barbra smiled. "We'll see."

◦৵৽◦

Creepers wasn't in the mood to play. He wanted to sit on my lap and have me pet him. Every time I tried to move, he would meow at me, and I'd feel guilty and stay. I sat on the window seat and looked out at the falling snow. It was my first winter in Kansas, and the snow was impressive. According to Boyd, we were getting a record-breaking amount his year. I'd stopped driving because driving through snow was not my talent.

My doorbell rang, and I glanced at the clock. 10:15 p.m. I put Creepers on the floor and walked down into the dining area of the restaurant. I could see Jett standing in the dark with snow falling around him.

I unlocked the door and peeked out. "Hey."

He grinned. "Hey. I stole your ladder."

"Boyd told me."

"I figured he would. I brought you a new one. It's out back in the shed. It's bigger and sturdier. That doesn't mean you should climb higher, though. You should hire someone to take care of your Christmas lights."

Creepers came over and wrapped himself around my ankles. Jett didn't look like he was moving, so I opened the door wider. "Do you want to come in?"

"Sure." He stepped in and took off his snowy boots.

I hugged myself and rubbed my cold arms. "Do you want some hot chocolate?"

"No, thanks. I just came to tell you that Silvia Clements wants me to come to her little party to make sure nothing goes wrong. She said you were catering. If you need any help, let me know. I can haul stuff in my truck if you need me to."

"Okay, thanks."

"She wants me to stay for three days. It seems a little excessive for a party."

"That's what I was thinking, but she's paying well. I'll leave Carrie in charge here. Between her and Tiffany, it should be fine for a few days." Carrie and Tiffany were sisters who both worked as cooks here. Tiffany was only part-time, but she'd agreed to work more this week.

"Ledford offered to go. I figured you wouldn't want to be stuck in a house with him for three days. He's particular about paperwork, so I told him to stay here and finish it how he likes it."

I was glad to hear that. Spending three days in the same house as Ledford might have been more than I could bear. He probably would hang around, making everyone un-comfortable.

"Besides," he said, "the Clements are paying me to do security, so I'm taking a few vacation days. I won't be on duty. That made Ledford mad as well, but since I've been sheriff, I've only taken two days off. I don't feel too bad about it."

"I'm sorry you didn't get a more—pleasant deputy."

Jett shrugged. "He's annoying, but he is helpful. It's better than not having a deputy." He told me about some things Ledford was doing, and I stopped listening. I got distracted by his three days' worth of stubble and thought back to my conversation with Boyd. I think Jett was the reason I suddenly liked stubble. He probably only shaved once or twice a week.

Jett rubbed his jaw. "Do I have something on my face?"

"Hmm?"

"You're staring at me funny."

My face felt hot, and I hoped the lighting was dim enough not to show my red face. "Sorry. I zoned out for a minute." I couldn't believe I was twenty-nine years old and still getting distracted by things like this.

"I know, I can get boring."

"No, you're not boring."

He grinned. "So what are you thinking that was more entertaining than my Ledford problems?"

There was no way I was telling him I would like nothing better than to kiss his jaw right now. "I just noticed you hadn't shaved for a few days. I was talking to Boyd about facial hair today, so it reminded me. Boyd wants to grow a goatee."

He chuckled. "I can see that." He rubbed his chin. "I should shave more."

I couldn't disagree without looking too invested.

"Hey, Barbra said you two found a will in the Clements's wardrobe. I wish she would have given it to me. I would have made sure it got to the right people, but she mailed it to them."

"I was hoping to find something more exciting, but it was still fun. It was mostly full of brand-new shoes. I wanted to find a treasure map or something."

"Finding a hidden will sounds exciting."

"It might have been, but it didn't say anything out of the ordinary."

"I was surprised Silvia Clements invited us to this thing. They never have people from Muddy Creek come. I think they feel they're too good for our small-town ways. I've never seen any of them in town before. They do all their shopping in bigger cities."

"I'm excited to see their house. Barbra said it's huge."

"Have you ever seen the outside?"

"No."

"It's impressive."

"I wonder why they want you there. It doesn't seem like the kind of event that would need law enforcement."

He shrugged. "They probably serve a lot of alcohol or something. They don't seem to be the type who would tolerate drunken brawls at their place."

"Have you ever met any of them?"

"I met Silvia and her brother Lionel at a charity event once. She was too good to talk to me, but I chatted with Lionel for a few minutes. He seemed nice enough. I haven't met any of their kids." He laughed. "It seems weird to call them kids. I think they're all in their forties."

"What's their house like?"

"I've only seen the outside, but it reminds me of Dracula's Castle. It's dark and, well, castle-ish."

I smiled. "Is castle-ish a word?"

"If it's not, it should be."

Creepers meowed at me. I picked him up. "He's needy today."

"I'll let you go. I shouldn't drop by so late."

"It's fine. I'll see you tomorrow."

I watched him walk out to his snow-covered truck, and I sighed. Solving mysteries was one of my skills, so why couldn't I solve the mystery of why I couldn't let the guy I liked know I liked him? I was almost positive he liked me. He'd given enough hints, but I always got scared and pretended not to notice.

I took Creepers up to our room and sat back on the window seat. "Why am I such a wimp?" I asked my cat. He purred on my lap. I knew why. Letting Jett know how much I liked him would be awkward if he didn't feel the same. Just guessing he did wasn't enough. I also had the nagging thought that he might only spend time around me because there weren't many single women under the age of fifty in Muddy Creek.

Chapter 3

Breakfast the following morning was busy. A tour bus had come through and hadn't called ahead, so everyone was working as fast as they could. The people had been kind enough to agree to eat waffles and bacon so we could make it in large batches. By the time the diner slowed down, it was 11:30.

I dropped down on a stool in the kitchen and pulled off my hairnet. My blond hair fell around my shoulders, and I yawned. It was going to be a long day.

"Silvia Clements sent me the menu for next week," José told me. "It shouldn't be too bad."

"How many people are we feeding?" I asked.

"Twenty-five people for nine meals."

"Will we have enough food?"

"It won't be a problem."

Carrie looked over from where she was washing a pan. Her brown hair was in a tight bun, and she looked tired. "I'm glad I don't have to go. I'd hate to cook for people like that. I'd be nervous and burn everything."

"I'm not worried," José said. "I thrive under pressure."

"It's good someone does," I said, looking out the serving window. Boyd sat at one table eating a waffle, and the rest of the room was empty. Boyd showed up most days even though it meant riding his electric bike through the deep snow.

I heard the front door open, and Jett and Deputy Ledford entered. Ledford's dark mustache reminded me of a bad guy in an old movie. It curled up slightly and looked like he put wax in it. They sat at Boyd's table and began talking quietly.

"I've got it," I said. Ledford's insistence on only getting dessert here was awkward for the servers. Once he knew lawmen got it free, it was all he ordered. I grabbed a notepad and walked into the dining area.

"Hello," I said. "What can I get you all today?"

Jett smiled. "I'll just have some hot chocolate and a scone."

"Does hot chocolate count as a dessert?" Ledford asked.

Jett rolled his eyes. "It counts as a drink."

"I'll have water and a cinnamon roll."

I jotted it down and tried to keep smiling. Ledford hadn't paid for anything since the first day he came here, and he came in almost every day. He prided himself on working the system.

"Do you need anything else, Boyd?"

"Nope. I'm good."

I nodded and walked away. I could hear Boyd talking behind me. "You shaved, Sheriff. That's probably why Ivy didn't hang around longer. She likes a man with a few days of stubble on his face."

I was horrified and kept walking.

Jett chuckled. "And she told you this?"

"Yep."

I hurried into the kitchen and handed the pad to one of the servers.

"Can someone take that out to Jett and Ledford?" I didn't wait for an answer. I grabbed my coat and went out the back door. I needed to go for a walk so I wouldn't say anything I might regret to Boyd.

My cute new boots weren't as sensible as I thought they would be. The fake fur around the top got wet every time I wore them and felt gross against my leg. When I'd seen them at the store, I'd gotten so excited I bought them without thinking. They were my first pair of winter boots. They might not be practical, but they were stylish. I walked around the town square, enjoying the cool air.

"Ivy Clark!" I turned and saw a woman rushing toward me. She'd pulled her hood over her head and wore a scarf over her mouth and nose. All I could see were her eyes, so I wasn't sure who she might be.

"Hello," I said as she approached me.

"Have you seen Jett?" she asked. "I don't get to town often, and I need to load up his truck so we'll be prepared for this next snowstorm. It's supposed to be a big one." It was Jett's mom. I thought her name might be Carol, but I'd only met her once on Thanksgiving.

"He's inside the diner."

"Does he eat there often? I feel guilty he isn't getting a lot of home-cooked meals now that he lives in town. We're too far for him to come every day with his job and all." She laughed. "I'm sure a can of soup tastes better than what I make. I hate cooking, but I'm willing to do it for the ones I love."

"He eats there a few times a week."

"Good. José is a superb cook. I could eat his food every day if I could get here. I keep telling my husband we should move to town. We don't have a lot going on at the farm, so it gets a bit lonely. Should we go join him? I could go for a cup of hot cocoa."

"He's with people," I said. "I'd love to sit with you and have a hot chocolate, though."

Mrs. Malone linked her arm with mine, and we walked toward the diner. "Who is he with?"

"Deputy Ledford and Boyd."

"I haven't met the deputy yet. I haven't heard a lot of good things about him."

I tilted my head. "He takes some getting used to."

We entered the diner and sat at a table. Mrs. Malone waved at Jett, and he waved back. He wore a small frown. Trina came over to take our order. Mrs. Malone ordered a hot chocolate and a piece of pie. I just got hot chocolate.

She smiled. "Jett looks uneasy. He's worried about what I might say to you. He'll be over here within five minutes to make sure I don't embarrass him."

I grinned, and Jett rubbed his lips together. He did look nervous.

"That Jett is a good kid. I'm proud of all he does around here. I know he'd rather work in a larger area, but he came here because he knew the town needed him. It's hard to have to arrest people he knows personally."

"I bet."

She laughed. "He always wanted to be a cop. When he was seven, he dressed like a police officer for Halloween. He tried to arrest his schoolteacher for giving him too much homework. He thought his little fake badge gave him authority. The sheriff at the time took him to his office and sat him down, and explained what it took to become a real lawman. He took it all to heart."

I smiled and looked at Jett. He stood and came to our table. "What's going on, Ma?"

"I'm having hot cocoa with Ivy."

"What are you talking about?"

"You, of course."

Jett sat next to me and frowned at his mom. "That's what I was afraid of."

"I haven't said anything bad, have I, Ivy?"

"Nope."

"I haven't even pulled out any pictures. If you ever want to see them, I have a whole stack of scrapbooks at my house. Drop by anytime."

I smiled at Jett. I would love to see his baby pictures.

Trina approached, putting our hot chocolates down along with Mrs. Malone's pie. "Is there anything else you need?"

"Nope. Thanks, Trina," Jett's mom said. She turned to Jett. "You're welcome to go back to your friends."

Jett shook his head. "Not a chance. I want to be able to defend myself."

She winked at him and took a bite of pie. It surprised me that people were still ordering pie. I thought of pie as a Thanksgiving-only thing, but we still sold some whenever it was on the menu.

"How is your expansion coming?" Mrs. Malone asked.

I perked up. The expansion was something I could talk about all day. "It's going well. We'll be able to use the extra space in the kitchen soon, and José will have an office to do all the paperwork in."

"And you're adding to your living quarters?"

"Yes. It will be as big as the downstairs when they're done. I'll have a kitchen, a living room, another bedroom, and a bathroom. That will be nice when my mom comes to visit."

"That will be nice."

"I'll also have a door that goes in from the back. That way, my visitors won't have to go through the diner." I was talking too much. Mrs. Malone didn't care about my expansion. She was just being polite.

"That will be nice. It will make them feel more separate. Have you seen Jett's house?" she asked.

"No."

"He's done a lot of work to it. Jett's always been into big trees. I don't think he saw anything when he went to look at the house except the big willow tree out front. He bought it just for that, I think."

Jett grinned. "It is a great tree. If you're only talking about boring things, I'm going to go save Boyd from Ledford." He stood and returned to his booth.

"That Jett really is a good kid. I hope he finds some time to have fun."

"I'm sure he does."

Chapter 4

The Clementses' kitchen was the biggest one I'd ever been in. Christmas decorations covered the walls, and bells with bows hung on the refrigerator handles and all the drawers. The double doors boasted two wreaths, and holly decorated all four corners. Since the holiday had passed, I wasn't in a Christmas mood, but it was fancy.

It shouldn't be surprising. I was shocked when I pulled up to the house. It was the biggest house I'd ever seen. It almost looked like a castle with its turrets and balconies. If I were wealthy, this wasn't the house I would choose. I couldn't help but be reminded of a vampire movie by the dark brick exterior. Jett had been right. I could imagine Dracula living here. I would hate to pull up to it in the dark.

I stood at the kitchen island and mixed frosting as fast as my arms would go. I hate mixing by hand, but I like the consistency better. These cinnamon rolls needed to be perfect. The Clementses were the most high-profile clients we could ever imagine, so making them happy was my top priority.

The door swung open, and José burst through carrying an armload of Tupperware. "It's cold outside." He shivered, placing it on the counter. "Boyd and Jett have the rest of the things we forgot."

"Oh good. I thought I had everything packed up last night. I can't believe how much I forgot."

"Who's watching Creepers?"

"Brian." Brian is the town librarian who gave me Creepers.

José walked up to me and gave me a peck on the cheek. My eyes widened, but I kept stirring. José and I are good friends, but I didn't realize we were greet-with-a-kiss type of friends.

"Is Anton here yet?" I asked.

"He's with Boyd."

"I'm really nervous. This could open a lot of opportunities for us."

José opened a container and took out a box of baking soda. "Don't stress. That's the most important thing. If we never get hired again, it's fine. Sue's Diner is doing fine without these gigs."

"I know. I just want it to be perfect."

Boyd and Anton came in, talking and laughing. Boyd put a bottle of vanilla on the island next to me and kissed my cheek. I stopped stirring and turned to question him, but Anton took my hand and kissed the back. My eyes narrowed. I didn't know what these three were up to, but I wouldn't let them get me riled up.

"Did you see the snowflakes?" Boyd asked. "Those things are huge! I hope we don't get snowed in. Where's Jett? I thought he came in ahead of me."

"I haven't seen him," I said.

"He's in a bad mood today," Anton said. "I think Deputy Sheriff Ledford is driving him crazy."

I went back to my icing. I was doing my best not to let Deputy Ledford bother me. Some people have a knack for driving everyone mad, and Ledford was one of those people. He'd only been here a few months, and people were already hiding in doorways around town to avoid talking to him. I knew I wanted to hide every time he came into the diner.

Jett entered the kitchen, grumbling about having to remove his shoes. We had all been instructed to take off our shoes at the door, and even our socks were unacceptable. We'd been given a pair of fancy black house shoes that were more slick than I was comfortable with.

"I don't know why the Clementses need me to be here," Jett said, shaking the snow from his brown hair. He must have already left his coat at the door with his shoes, and he wore jeans and a black T-shirt. I tried not to notice how good he looked, but that was hard to do.

"It always throws me when you aren't wearing your sheriff clothes," Boyd said, grinning at him.

"The Clementses have a lot of rules. They gave me a typed list of what they expect from me, like I'm one of their employees. What to wear, how to stand. I hope they know I'm doing this as a service to them."

I'd rarely seen Jett annoyed like this. Ledford was really throwing off his moods. Jett was usually a laid-back guy.

Boyd grinned. "If you can see past your anger, you might realize something magical awaits you."

Anton snorted, and José chuckled as he poured something into a bowl. I just shook my head. I didn't see anything magical in the kitchen unless they meant the sparkling candles decorating the walls.

"What are you talking about?" Jett asked. "Ohhh."

I looked at Jett to see what everyone was talking about, but he was just smiling like a kid at Christmas.

"What?" I asked.

"She hasn't seen it yet," Boyd said. "You better move fast before she does."

I was too busy to figure out Boyd and his puzzles. The icing looked perfect.

Jett came over and stood in front of me, still smiling. "I've been waiting a long time for this."

I looked in the bowl. "For icing or cinnamon rolls?"

Jett pointed up at the ceiling. I looked up, and my mouth fell open as I spotted the mistletoe. How had I missed that?

Before I could escape, Jett grabbed my arms. I wished he would quit smiling at me like that. My heart pounded so hard I was sure everyone in the room could hear it. He wouldn't really kiss me in front of my crew, would he? I was terrified he would and terrified he wouldn't. I'd been dreaming about kissing Jett for a long time. And not the kind of kiss José, Boyd, or Anton had given me.

Before I could go into a full-on panic, Jett leaned down and pressed his lips softly against mine. I heard the others clap, but it was only background noise. Jett began to pull away, but that wasn't how our first kiss was going to go. I'd been waiting too long. I wrapped my arms around his neck and pulled him closer. His arms encircled me, and I ignored the cheering.

My stomach twisted and turned, and the panic returned. Once we broke the kiss, then what? Everything goes back to normal? Everyone knew mistletoe didn't mean anything. It was just a silly tradition. A silly, perfect tradition. Who was supposed to stop the kiss? There was too much about relationships and kissing that I didn't have much experience with. Not that we had a relationship. And what were my hands doing in the back of his hair?

Boyd chuckled. "I think that's overdoing it for mistletoe. You two are embarrassing Anton."

I pulled away and turned, not wanting to see Jett's face. He'd meant it to be a soft, fast kiss, and I'd been ridiculous. Not only that, but I'd done it in front of everyone. I walked over to the tall upright freezer and opened it, blocking everyone's view of me. With luck, the icy air would help cool my face.

I assumed from the sound that someone was clapping Jett on the back. I rolled my eyes. I wished they would all go away. While I was wishing, I wished Jett would come over and kiss me again. I shook my head and wondered how long I could stay over here before someone came to see if I'd died or something. They were all talking, but I couldn't tell what they were saying.

"Do you think we have enough eggnog?" I asked, trying to sound normal.

"Plenty," José assured.

"Why don't you come back over here, Ivy?" Jett asked.

I closed my eyes and kept myself hidden.

Boyd laughed. "You can't stay in the freezer forever."

"Yes, I can."

They all laughed.

Jett peeked around the freezer, and I refused to acknowledge him. "That's some interesting ice you're watching in there."

I frowned. The only thing in the enormous freezer was bags and bags of ice, and I'd been staring at them for three minutes. Jett rested his hand on the top of the freezer door. I didn't know what to do or say, so I just stood there, ignoring the fact that Jett was staring at me, and I was staring at the ice.

Jett released the door, then took my arm, moved me gently away from the freezer, and shut the door. The kitchen was empty except for the two of us. That was just great. That meant the others had all frantically motioned to each other to leave the two of us alone. They were probably in the hallway, listening at the door.

"You aren't going to let things get weird between us now, are you?" he asked.

"Of course not," I lied. "I just have a lot to get done. It's like you said. The Clementses have high expectations, and I have a lot to get done." Great. I'd just repeated myself.

He crossed his arms and leaned against the counter. "And staring at the ice is one of those things you have to get done?"

"I was just thinking for a minute. I can't believe I didn't see that mistletoe. I should have known something was up when the others kissed me."

Jett frowned. "What others?"

"José, Boyd, and Anton."

"They all kissed you?" His eyes narrowed.

I rolled my eyes and walked back to the island. "On the cheek and hand." I grabbed the already mixed icing and began mixing it again.

"And she walks right back under the mistletoe."

My eyes went wide as I realized my mistake. I hugged my bowl against me and took it to the other end of the island.

Jett walked slowly toward me. "I thought you were sending me an invitation."

Butterflies stormed my stomach, and I tried to glare at him. I hoped it was a glare and not a look pleading for him to come closer. He continued to approach, so I wasn't sure. He took the bowl from my hands and put it on the island.

I pointed up. "No mistletoe."

Jett smiled, then wrapped his arms around my waist and picked me up. A small squeak slipped from my mouth, and my hands gripped his shoulders so I wouldn't fall. He carried me to the other side of the island and put me back on my feet.

"Problem solved."

I forced myself to look up at him and not pass out. I thought about making a joke and walking away, but that would mean missing out on what I really wanted. Being horrible at these things was the reason I was almost thirty, and I'd only had one relationship that had barely lasted. I was very aware of the fact that Jett's arms were still around me.

"Once more, and I'll never ask again," Jett said. I frowned. That wasn't what I wanted. He grinned. "I mean, I'll never ask to kiss you in the Clementses' kitchen again."

My arms were ahead of my mind, and they went up and rested on his upper arms. That must have been all the invitation Jett needed because he kissed me again. The first kiss had nothing on this one. I could feel my arms shaking, and I hoped he didn't notice. If I could get my stomach to stop flipping, that would have been nice. My hands moved up and found his hair again. I didn't realize how much I liked Jett's hair until today.

Something in the back of my mind told me I was supposed to be doing something, but I wasn't sure what. Did anything besides what I was doing actually matter? Jett broke the kiss, and I did my best not to feel disappointed.

He smiled at me and winked. "I better go find the others and let them know it's safe to return." I watched him leave the kitchen.

I leaned back against the island and put a hand to my heart. Kissing Jett was even better than I'd imagined, and now I would have to pretend I didn't care. The door opened, and I rushed over to the oven to check the cinnamon rolls. Anton, Boyd, and José entered and got to work. None of them said anything, which seemed out of character.

I pulled the cinnamon rolls from the oven and smiled. They smelled perfect. I placed them on the island to cool.

"I'll be surprised if most of the guests don't cancel," Anton said. "The snow is coming down really hard."

"I hope we don't get snowed in," Boyd said.

José nodded as he seasoned the meat. "If we do, at least we were already planning to stay for three days."

"The weatherman said it's going to get worse," Anton said. "It's the most snow we've had in over twenty years."

It seemed strange to hear everyone talking like it was a perfectly normal day. There was nothing normal about it. This was the day Sheriff Jett Malone had finally kissed me.

Chapter 5

The door to the Clementses' kitchen opened, and a woman entered. I couldn't place her age. She looked to be in her fifties, but she'd had plastic surgery. Her brown hair was curled and fell just past her shoulders, and her makeup was perfect. She wore a long blue evening gown and a diamond necklace and earrings. Her eyes narrowed as she watched us.

"I'm Ivy Clark," I said, walking up and holding out my hand. "I'm the owner of Sue's Diner."

She barely touched my hand, then wiped her palm on her dress. "Silvia Clements. I'm sure you already know that. I wasn't thrilled to hire a diner to cater our biggest party of the year, but our regular caterer fell through at the last moment. Everyone else worth having was booked."

I tried to keep my face passive. "Thanks for giving us this opportunity."

She sighed. "Who is the head chef?"

"This is José," I said, motioning to José. He smiled from where he was stirring something on the stove.

"It's nice to meet you," he said.

Silvia frowned. "Let me get someone to translate." She opened the door and yelled, "Maria!"

"Why do you need a translator?" I asked.

"So I can make sure the instructions I give to the cook are clear. We can't have any mistakes, and he'll understand better in his own language."

José's eyes narrowed. "English is my language."

"Maria!" she yelled again. A woman about my age entered the kitchen and bowed her head to Silvia. Her long black hair was pulled back in a ponytail, and she wore a black dress and a white apron just like a maid would in a movie.

"Yes, Madam?" the woman said with a Spanish accent.

Silvia pointed at José. "Tell this man that I expect everything to go perfectly this week."

The woman turned to José and said something in Spanish.

José crossed his arms, and I hoped he would remain polite even though this woman was awful.

Silvia nodded. "Tell him he will never get another job in the cooking industry if he fails."

The woman said something else.

José shook his head. "I don't speak Spanish."

Silvia ignored him. "We expect dinner exactly at six o'clock." Maria fiddled with her hands and looked from José to Silvia. "Well, tell him!"

Maria took a deep breath and spouted off more Spanish.

José looked at me, and I shrugged.

"Dinner will be ready at six o'clock," José said. "And it will be perfect."

Silvia looked at Maria. "Well? What did he say?"

Maria blinked twice. "Dinner will be ready at six o'clock, and it will be perfect."

"Wonderful," Silvia said. She turned and left the room.

Maria stood still for a moment, then walked timidly up to José. "I'm sorry. There's no point in arguing with her once she gets something in her head."

José smiled. "Don't worry about it."

She nodded and hurried from the room.

Anton grinned. "That Silvia seems like a ray of sunshine. It's no wonder they stay away from town. I bet they're way too good for a place like Muddy Creek."

"Just do your best to fly under the radar," I suggested as I grabbed a cutting board.

"It's going to make a good story," Anton said. "I can already tell."

I grabbed a tomato, then cut it and tossed it in the salad. "How long until six o'clock?"

"About an hour," José said.

The door burst open, and Jett came through. "That woman is impossible!" he whisper-yelled.

I laughed. "We agree."

"She wants me to walk around the entire perimeter of the property every fifteen minutes until eleven thirty. She's crazy if she thinks someone will crash her party in this weather. I'll be shocked if anyone can get down the road. Someone plowed the driveway, but the road looks bad."

"So none of the guests will make it?" I asked.

"I doubt it. One couple is already here, but I'll be shocked if anyone else gets through."

A man walked in, and they all fell silent. He looked like he was in his upper sixties. He wore a tux and had a comb-over. The man walked to the fridge, not acknowledging anyone, and pulled out a bottle of wine. He popped it open and began drinking from the bottle. Jett's eyes narrowed as the man drank half the bottle, then stuck it back in the fridge.

I tried not to stare as he kicked the fridge shut and left the room.

Jett came over and stood next to me. "That was Clint Stetson. He's Silvia's husband. She was bossing him around a minute ago."

I kept cutting tomatoes and ignoring how close Jett was to me. "I was excited about this, but now I'm a little nervous."

Jett put his hand on my back. "It'll be fine. Once they eat José's food, everyone will be in a good mood."

Boyd was sitting at the island on a stool doing a crossword. I wasn't sure why he was even here, but he'd insisted on coming. He turned and grinned. "We don't need to leave the kitchen again, do we?"

Jett dropped his hand, and I dumped the last of the tomatoes into the salad and took the cutting board to the sink.

Now the cinnamon rolls were cool, I could add the icing. I grabbed the bowl and frowned when I looked at it. I would never see icing again without thinking about kissing Jett.

"Should I drizzle the icing or spread it?" I asked.

"I like it spread," Jett said. "It tastes better."

"Drizzling looks fancy, though," said José, "and I think these people are going for fancy."

José was right. Drizzling it would look more impressive, but limit the amount I could put on.

Maria came back into the kitchen. She grabbed a rag from a drawer and went to the sink to get it wet. A man in his early forties entered and came up behind her. He wore a tux like Clint, and his brown hair was neatly parted on the side. They began having a whispered conversation.

I knew it wasn't polite to listen, so I tried to ignore them as I drizzled icing across the rolls.

"No!" Maria said loudly. Everyone paused, then went back to what they were doing. "You're a forty-year-old man! If you can't stand up to your own mother, then I have nothing to say to you." She stomped from the room, and the man sighed and followed.

I looked at Jett. "Silvia's son?"

"Yeah. His name's Kyle. He was bothering a different maid when I saw him earlier. I better go out and patrol the area."

I watched him leave. "Poor Jett," I said, icing a roll. "It's freezing out there."

Boyd grinned. "Poor Jett? I'm sure he's glad he's here. That mistletoe made it all worth it. Now he has something nice to think about while he's freezing his toes off."

Anton snorted, and José chuckled quietly.

I gave Boyd my best glare. "Not funny. And you know, what happens in the Clementses' kitchen stays in the Clementses' kitchen."

Boyd threw his head back and laughed. I could hear the others chuckling, but I didn't look at them. "You can fire Anton and José, but not me."

I shook my head and kept drizzling.

"You know we're just having fun with you," Boyd said. "And it is about time the two of you changed your relationship."

"Nothing's changed," I protested. "It's just mistletoe. It doesn't count for anything."

Boyd raised his brow. "And what happened when we all left the room?"

José grinned. "Cut it out, Boyd. We've embarrassed her enough for one day."

"Don't give me that," Boyd said. "You know you want to know as much as I do. Any more kissing?"

I placed the iced cinnamon rolls on a platter and moved it to the table. "I'm not talking to you, Boyd."

He laughed and slapped his leg. "I'll take that as a yes."

My insides fluttered, and I told myself to stop being ridiculous. Jett wasn't even in the room, for goodness' sake. I wasn't counting those kisses as anything that might be meaningful to Jett until he told me that himself. I would probably spend all night trying not to think about the entire thing.

I grabbed some empty bins and decided to take them to my car to get them out of the way. I struggled when I tried to open the front door.

"Let me help you with that," the butler said, rushing over and opening the door. He wasn't what I would have pictured as a butler. He was around forty-five and about six-foot-one. His black suit and green tie were perfectly pressed, and his shoes shined black. He was attractive, with dark brown hair and an impressive shoulder span. Not as notable as Jett's, but no one would win compared to him.

"Thank you," I said as I walked out the door. He took some of the containers from the top of my pile and carried them to my car.

"I'm Eric Daniels, if you don't remember," he said. "I'm the one who let you in when you arrived."

"Oh yes. And I'm Ivy."

"Yes. I've been to Sue's Diner. It's a lovely place you have there."

"Thank you."

"I don't get out much, but when I do, I like small-town diners."

My feet were freezing, so I looked down. "Oh no. I wore the slippers out here, and so did you."

He chuckled. "There are plenty, believe me. We can switch them out when we get back in. Silvia doesn't have to know."

I should have worn my coat. It was almost impossible to see through the blowing snow.

"Does Silvia own the house?" I asked, popping the trunk and tossing in the containers.

He frowned as he put his stack in. "Yes. When Zeb Clements died, he left most of his wealth to Silvia. He left a little for the rest of his family, but she got the largest amount and most of the shares in the family company."

I slammed the trunk, and we went back to the house. I shivered as we entered. A wooden box with flowers carved on top sat near the door. Eric opened it and took off his slippers, then tossed them in the box. I followed his lead. He opened a nearly identical box next to it, pulled out a fresh pair, and handed them to me. I put them on my cold, wet feet.

"Does the entire family live here?" I asked, realizing I was prying.

"Yes. Silvia and her husband, Clint, have the upper floor. Their son, Kyle, comes and goes. Then Silvia's brother, Lionel, and his wife live on the middle floor with their two adult daughters."

"And they aren't married?" I grinned. "Sorry. I'm too nosy."

He smiled. "Not at all. I imagine everyone in Muddy Creek is curious about the Clementses. They aren't very neighborly. And no, Lionel's daughters aren't married."

The door opened, and Jett came in. He removed his boots and put them on a shoe rack in a large closet near the door, then pulled on some black slippers.

"I probably shouldn't tell you this, Sheriff," Eric said, "but it's a waste of time to patrol the property. We have enough security, and with the snow, no one's going to come around. Silvia will never know you aren't doing it if you stay out of sight."

"I don't mind once or twice an hour, but four is a little excessive," Jett said, taking off his heavy blue coat.

"Silvia won't notice. She's angry enough right now at her guests for canceling. I'm afraid there will be a lot of leftover food," Eric said.

"Can the staff eat it?" I asked. I wasn't worried about me. Silvia had already paid me in full, so I wouldn't lose anything.

Eric rolled his eyes. "She'll let us eat any remaining food in the kitchen after dinner, but Silvia doesn't believe in keeping leftovers. She'll toss them."

Jett shook his head. "That's a shame. José is an excellent cook."

"I have a small fridge in my room. I could put the leftovers in there and share them with the others. Most of the staff is off right now. There are only three of us. The Clementses let the cooks and most of the others take January off, so it's quiet around here."

The time for being nosy was over. I had a deadline. "I better get back to the kitchen," I said. "It's almost time to begin serving."

Chapter 6

Eric held the dining room door open, and Maria and another maid named Callie carried trays of food into the room. I walked behind them, carrying the gravy. Silvia didn't want José, Boyd, or Anton coming out of the kitchen, so another trip would be needed to give everyone their plates.

I placed the gravy on the table where I'd been instructed and stepped back. Eight people sat at a table that was supposed to hold over twenty. Silvia was smiling, but I could tell she was annoyed by how tightly she held her lips. What was she expecting? The weather was horrid.

A large Christmas tree decorated in silver and gold stood in one corner. The tablecloth was gold and so were the plates. Two women in their forties sat together, whispering. They must be Lionel's daughters. They were dressed as fancy as their aunt, Silvia, with their long gowns and fancy updos. One had brown hair, and the other brownish red. They were both looking at something past Ivy. She glanced back and saw Eric. He was frowning.

A couple about Silvia's age sat across from them. They must be the guests who arrived early. Callie and Maria left the room, and I followed. Eric pulled the door shut and let out a breath. He muttered something, and we all followed him back to the kitchen.

"This is ridiculous," Callie said. "Silvia's still acting like the queen even though there isn't anyone to impress."

Eric nodded. "Don't worry. She'll get hers, eventually. Her type always does."

Callie rubbed her shoulder. "I've worked here too long."

"We all have," Eric stated.

"I've been here sixteen years!" Callie announced as they entered the kitchen. "I started when I was twenty and haven't been happy since."

"So quit," Maria said, walking to the island and picking up another tray. Callie grasped the last one, and they followed Eric back out the door.

Jett sat in a chair in the corner, eating a cinnamon roll. I sat in the chair beside him and whispered, "Something's weird with the Clementses."

He nodded. "There's a lot wrong with them, and I'm saying this after only knowing them for half a day."

"When Barbra and I discovered Zeb's will, we read he had specified an equal division of his possessions between his children and grandchildren."

"Makes sense."

"Eric just said that Silvia inherited almost everything. The will had a sticky note that said Zeb was worried someone might mess with his will."

"Hmm," Jett said, wiping his fingers on a napkin. "I wish Barbra had given me the will. I'll have to look into it when I get back to my office."

"I took a picture of it. I'll text it to you." I took out my phone and scrolled to the picture and sent it.

"That's helpful. It'll be hard to read on my phone, but I'll look at it when I get to a computer."

I nodded and went to help José and Anton clean up.

"Where's Boyd?" I asked.

"He went to bed," Anton said.

"Already?"

José grinned. "Boyd said that one of the highlights of being old is you can sleep whenever you want."

❦

The room I was staying in was bigger and nicer than my entire living space at the diner. The room had three lights, all adorned with crystal-covered covers. The bed was so comfortable that I could see myself staying in it forever.

The heavy blue quilt was soft and warm, and I curled up underneath it. It didn't matter how comfortable the bed was, I couldn't sleep. I couldn't help but divide my thoughts between remembering kissing Jett and contemplating Zeb Clements's will.

Silvia must have altered the will. No one else would have a motive to give her everything. Well, maybe her husband. Her son, Kyle, wouldn't have a reason to help her. He would have gotten more money with the original will.

I'd thought about this over and over, and I wasn't coming up with anything different than I had an hour ago. My mind slipped back to Jett, and I touched my lips. I still couldn't believe he did that in front of everyone. I smiled. Maybe I could. It was embarrassing but worth it.

Arguing in the hall drew my attention. I crept out of bed and made my way to the door. I pressed my ear against it and tried to listen.

"You make promises, promises, promises, and you never come through." I recognized Maria's accent.

"I'm sorry," Kyle said. "It's just my mom. She's never going to accept us."

"You said you didn't care. You're a liar."

"Come on, Maria. Don't be like this. We're going to make it work."

"You know I've only stayed working here for you? I hate it here. Your mother is a monster to work for."

"I know," Kyle said. "My mom is ridiculous, but I have a plan. I'm going to take care of everything."

"I've heard that before. I've heard it for years. This is your last chance. If you don't tell your parents about us by the end of the week, I'm leaving."

I felt guilty for listening, but I couldn't make myself go back to bed.

"If my mom finds out about us, it's over. She'll cut me off, then what? Give me more time. Everyone knows my grandpa had another will. I need to find it."

I frowned. If Barbra sent the will when she said she did, it should have gotten here by now. That meant it hadn't or someone hadn't shared its arrival with everyone.

"I'm sick of hearing about the will. If it was here, you would have found it by now."

"I'll find it. I'll go right now and search through all my grandfather's things again."

"Fine. But if you don't find it, I'm leaving."

I could hear footsteps going in two directions. I grabbed my pink robe and pulled it over my nightshirt, then carefully opened the door. Kyle disappeared around the corner, and Maria around another. Running on my bare toes, I followed Kyle. If I could see where Zeb's old room was, I could come back later and search it myself.

I peeked around the corner and watched him go up a large red-carpeted staircase. There was a large room around the staircase that looked like an entryway, but it was in the middle of the house.

This house had too many staircases. I hadn't seen most of the house, but I'd already seen three. Following him would be too obvious. I waited until he disappeared, and I scurried up the stairs. The hallway went straight, and Kyle stood in the dim pathway. I dropped down on the stairs and listened.

A door creaked. "Kyle, what are you doing?" Silvia asked. I peeked over the top of the step and saw Silvia peering out of what must be her bedroom.

Kyle let go of the door he was about to open. "I couldn't sleep."

"Well, come in here. I need to talk to you about some things."

Kyle hung his head. "Yes, Mother."

I shook my head. Forty years old and still not his own man. He disappeared inside, and I decided to take my chance. I rushed over to the room that must be Zeb's and turned the knob. It opened quietly, and I entered, closing it softly.

The room was dark, and I didn't dare turn on the light. I didn't have my phone, so I had no light. I walked carefully over to the window and opened the blinds. There wasn't much light, but the outside of the house had a lot of lights, so it was better than nothing.

The room had an enormous bed and some other furniture I couldn't clearly make out. This was ridiculous. I wasn't going to find anything like this. Even a flashlight would be too small to be helpful. Moving around the room, I touched the walls. I came to a stop upon reaching a door. I yanked it open and squinted, struggling to glimpse what was inside. It was too dark, but I was sure it was a closet.

It was surprising to find Zeb still had a room here. When Barbra said there had been an estate sale after he died, I'd figured they sold all his things.

My heart stopped when I heard the doorknob turn. I jumped into the closet and silently closed the door. I stepped back until I hit the wall. There weren't any clothes or anything else I could find to hide behind. I breathed through my nose and tried not to make any sound. I shifted on my cold feet and listened.

Someone was walking around. The footsteps sounded slow and deliberate. No light had shone from under the closet door, so whoever was in here hadn't switched on the lights. That meant whoever was in here shouldn't be.

The footsteps were getting closer. I tried to come up with a clever excuse for being here, but I had nothing. The closet door opened slowly, and I held my breath. The silhouette of a man stood peering into the closet. I couldn't make out who he was. The bedroom doorknob sounded again, and he stepped into the closet and shut the door.

I let out a slow, silent breath. I was hiding in a closet with someone who didn't know I was here. It might be Kyle, but wouldn't he turn on the light? Whoever it was didn't want to be found any more than I did. How did I get myself into these kinds of things? If he moved, he might bump into me.

Light shone under the closet door, and I cringed. Someone walked around the room, then the light went off, and the door slammed. The sound of a key turning in a lock made me frown. Now I was locked in this room with someone. I thought about screaming and hoping it scared him, but I couldn't count on it.

"Ivy?" Jett said quietly next to me.

I jumped, then punched him in the arm. At least I think it was in the arm.

"What was that for?" he asked.

"You scared me to death!" I said quietly. "I thought I was hiding in here with Kyle!"

He chuckled under his breath. "I wondered what you were thinking."

"How did you find me?"

"I saw you sneaking up the stairs, so I followed you."

"My heart is beating so hard right now! Why didn't you tell me it was you when you opened the closet?"

"I couldn't see anything. I don't have my phone. I knew you must be hiding in the room somewhere, but then I heard someone opening the door, so I jumped in."

"My hands are shaking."

"That's what happens when you sneak around." I could hear the smile in his voice.

"Why are we still in the closet?"

"I dunno. It's kind of nice, and dark, and closed in."

I shivered. "You're creeping me out. Now I feel like something's going to jump out and eat me."

"Really? Because that wasn't the direction I was going." He put his hands on my arms, and I froze. One of his hands found my face.

"What are you doing? There's no mistletoe." I wanted to bite my tongue the moment I said it. I would love nothing more than to stand in a dark closet kissing Jett.

"Mistletoe was invented by a coward."

"I think it grows on trees."

The next thing I knew, he was kissing me. I wrapped my arms around his neck and tried to calm the butterflies in my stomach. There were no prying eyes, just Jett and I. He pulled away too soon.

"I have a question," he said. I could feel his breath on my face. "I hope you'll give me an honest answer."

I swallowed and stared into the darkness. He was going to ask me if I liked him. How would I answer? I didn't want to answer something like that without knowing what he thought.

"I try to be honest," I managed. Our arms were still around each other, and it felt perfect.

"The apron I gave you. You hate it, don't you?"

I laughed softly. "That's not what I thought you were going to say."

"Tell me the truth. Or are you scared of me?"

"I'm not scared of you."

"Then tell me about the apron." I could hear the humor in his voice.

"It's the ugliest apron I've ever seen in my entire life."

"Oh yeah?"

"Absolutely hideous."

"Then why do you wear it so often?"

I ran my hands through the back of his hair, feeling bold in the darkness. "If you don't know, I'm not going to tell you." I leaned in and was relieved when my lips found his. Missing them would have ruined the moment.

Chapter 7

A piercing scream woke me from a deep slumber, causing me to sit up quickly in bed. I breathed deeply as I looked around the dark, unfamiliar room. I felt disoriented for a few moments, then remembered I was at the Clementses' house. Hopping out of bed, I slipped my feet into my house shoes and pulled my robe on.

I waited a moment, listening. I'd thought I heard a scream, but it was possibly part of my dream. I'd stayed up too late spying on Kyle and kissing Jett. We'd snuck out of the closet and carefully unlocked the door and gone our separate ways. It felt like a substantial amount of time had passed, but the clock showed it was only a little over two hours ago.

Another scream echoed through the house, and I ran out of my room and tried to see down the dark hallway.

It was too dark, and I didn't know where the light switch was. I returned to my room and flipped on the light. Nothing happened. The power must have gone out. I grabbed my phone and shook it, turning on the flashlight. I ventured back into the hallway and ran in the direction I'd heard the scream.

I rounded the corner and stopped when I reached the large staircase. I shined my light around and spotted Maria covering her face at the bottom of the stairs.

"What's wrong?" I asked as Jett ran into the area.

Maria pointed down. I shined my light on the floor. Silvia lay there, unmoving. I gasped, and Jett dropped to his knees. I kept my light focused on her. The area was soon filled with everyone from the house.

"Silvia!" Clint exclaimed, dropping down next to Jett.

"She's dead," Jett said.

"What!" someone cried.

Maria put a hand to her head. "I heard her fall down the stairs."

"We need more light," Jett announced.

"I have a lantern in my room," Eric offered, turning and running out of sight.

"Why isn't the generator working?" a woman asked. I couldn't tell whether it was Amanda or Jennifer.

Jett looked up. "José, call 911 and tell them to send an ambulance."

"I already tried. I'm not getting any service," José said.

"Neither am I," someone else said.

Eric came back with a lantern, bathing the area in dim light. It made shadows dance across the walls, and I felt a shiver go up my spine.

"She has a wound," Jett said. "I'm not sure what it's from."

A collective gasp sounded, and everyone started looking around nervously.

"Can anyone make a call?" Jett asked.

I turned off my light and looked at my phone. I had no service and no internet.

Jett sighed. "Great. I'll have to drive into town."

"There's no way," Eric said. "Have you looked outside? Even if you dig out a vehicle, it won't go anywhere."

Jett nodded. "Alright. I want everyone to go to their room and lock their doors. Do you understand?"

Everyone nodded or mumbled an agreement. I noticed there was a lack of tears from the group. Even Silvia's husband and son only looked slightly distressed. Perhaps it hadn't sunk in yet.

"Everyone stay in your rooms until morning. I'll come get you when I decide it's safe to come out, and I need to talk to you all, one at a time. José, can you help me?"

"Sure."

One by one, the family and employees left, leaving Jett, Boyd, and José. I wasn't going anywhere.

"Ivy, go to bed," Jett said.

I crossed my arms. "You know I can't."

"You were up late. You'll be more useful in the morning."

"No one's going to sleep after this. Everyone's probably in their room freaked out."

"Probably, but I need to know everyone is in their room. I can look around for any signs of forced entry."

"Who could have come in this storm? It's an inside job." I said it like it was a fact.

"Probably, but I need to know for sure. If there is an intruder, we have to be careful."

"Don't we have to be careful, regardless?" I asked. "If there's a killer, does it really matter if they came from inside or outside the house?"

José shrugged. "If it was someone here, I don't think anyone else is in danger. We've only been here one day, and I can already tell most of the people here hated Silvia."

"That's for sure. Her own son and husband didn't look more concerned than anyone else," Boyd said. "That makes them look a little guilty to me."

"I overheard Kyle and Maria talking," I said. "It sounds like they have a relationship that Silvia wouldn't approve of. Maria gave him an ultimatum."

"So it was Kyle," Boyd said. "Or Maria."

"Maybe," Jett said, still looking Silvia over. "But it could have something to do with the will. If Silvia changed the will, any of her family could be angry."

"You know," Boyd said, "now that I think about it, it was probably the butler. It's always the butler."

"Eric seems decent," I said.

"I don't know," José said. "Eric told Callie that Silvia would get hers."

I shook my head. "I don't think he meant it threateningly. He just meant rotten people can't stay that way without consequences forever."

"What do we need to do?" Boyd asked. "Should we move the body?"

Jett let out a slow breath. "I don't know. If we move her, we could destroy evidence, but we can't just leave a dead body here for everyone to walk by. Since we can't leave and can't call anyone, it's going to be messy. I don't want her moved until at least the morning when I can see better."

"Why were there two screams?" Boyd asked.

"I think Silvia was stabbed and then pushed down the stairs," Jett said. "My guess is the second scream was Maria when she found the body. I'll have to ask her to confirm. José, I want you to stay by the body. I'm going to go talk to everyone, one at a time."

"What about me?" I asked.

"You go to bed. You too, Boyd."

"You don't have to tell me twice," Boyd said.

Jett tilted his head. "Actually, I did."

Boyd chuckled and disappeared down the hall, using his phone as a light.

"You know I'm not going to sleep," I said. "What if I look outside for any weird prints in the snow?"

Jett frowned. "No. I need you to go to bed. Let me deal with this."

I took a deep breath and nodded.

José grinned. He looked scary with the lantern light bouncing off his face. "Come on, Jett. Give Ivy a job. If you don't, you know she'll be snooping around on her own."

Jett scratched the stubble on his chin, and I tried not to wish I was kissing him. "Stay here with José. I don't want anyone tampering with anything." He stood and went up the stairs, not waiting for an answer.

I crossed my arms and sat on a stair. "What he means is, sit here and let José babysit you."

José smiled. "Or maybe the other way around. You've gotten out of a lot more sticky situations than I ever have."

"Yes, but I cause most of them myself." We fell silent, and I tried not to be bothered by the fact I was in a dim area with a dead body. There was a crackling noise somewhere at the top of the stairs. It sounded like someone was opening a candy bar.

"Did you hear that?" I whispered.

José nodded. He stood and walked silently up the stairs. I turned and crawled silently after him. This was the second time tonight I'd hidden on these stairs.

José bent down when he got near the top and peeked over. "There's nobody there," he whispered.

I moved up next to him, and my eyes scanned the darkness. "How can you tell?"

"I can't see anyone."

"I can't see anything."

A door opened, and I sucked in a breath. Someone holding a flashlight exited the room and walked toward us. I turned and rushed down the stairs. I could hear José behind me. When I got to the bottom, I turned. Jett was walking down the stairs. I couldn't see his expression.

"What are you two doing?" he asked.

"We heard something," I said. "We were just seeing what it was."

"What was it?"

"We couldn't see anything."

Jett stepped into the dim light, and I saw his eyebrows rise. "Where's Silvia?"

I spun around and looked at the floor. All that was there was a small pool of blood. My eyes searched the rest of the area. Nothing.

"We were only at the top of the stairs for a minute!" I said. Jett walked around the area, shining his flashlight in all the corners. He ran into the hallway and vanished around the corner.

"Great," I muttered. "How could someone take a body and disappear that fast? And why?"

"Hide evidence?" José guessed.

"Maybe, but wouldn't that leave more evidence? We already know she's dead, and now they might have left more clues."

José looked around. "I bet Jett went the wrong way. There's no way someone took a body and got away that fast. They must have hidden it or gone out the window or something."

"We would have heard the window open and close. Someone strong might have thrown the body over their shoulder and ran."

"It would be hard to get far like that."

I sighed. "I can't believe I let Jett down like this."

Chapter 8

My eyes felt dry, and I struggled to keep them open. I should have stayed in bed. As far as I could tell, I was the only one awake. When I accepted this job, one condition was serving breakfast at exactly seven o'clock. Sure, the person who'd ordered that was dead, but I'd been paid and would do what was expected.

I cracked some eggs in a bowl and whisked them. The power had come back on, but not the phone service. Making regular meals isn't my talent, but I would do my best and let the others get some needed sleep. I make a killer dessert, but my skills are limited outside of that. The door creaked open, and José entered. He yawned and frowned when he spotted me.

"What are you doing to my breakfast?"

I tilted my head. "Making it."

José took the bowl and whisk from me. "I appreciate the thought, but I've got it."

What he was saying was that I should stick to my desserts. That was what I excelled at. Since breakfast rarely came with dessert, I had nothing to do. I sat on a stool at the island and rested my face against my hand.

This job had turned into a disaster. I wondered if people would start avoiding me. How could so many weird things happen around me? Jett had searched the entire house last night and hadn't found Silvia's body. At three in the morning, we had all admitted defeat and gone to bed. Three hours of sleep wasn't enough.

Jett entered. He wore jeans and a green polo shirt. He looked more awake than seemed possible after the night he'd had.

"Hey, Ivy?" he said. "Can I talk to you for a minute?"

Great. This was going to be the lecture I knew was coming. Shouldn't José share it? He'd lost the body too, after all.

"Sure," I said, following him out the door. He led me through the hallway and into the large entryway near the front door. "I can give myself the lecture."

He studied me. "What lecture?"

"I should have watched the body better."

"That's not what I wanted to talk about. Accidents happen."

"Then what is it?"

"Last night, I talked to everyone in the house. No one gave me anything to go on. They all said the same thing. They were asleep; they heard the scream; they ran to see what happened. I didn't see a single tear from anyone."

I frowned. I hadn't enjoyed being around Silvia, but it was sad no one seemed upset by her death.

"I'm not sure whether the people here know about your experience of solving these sorts of things. If they don't, you might be able to talk to them better than I can. Maybe get some answers."

I smiled. "Are you asking me to help you solve a case?"

He grinned. "It sounds like it. Be careful, though. Make sure everyone you talk to knows that someone else knows you are talking to them."

"And take Boyd?" I was used to everyone telling me to take Boyd every time I did anything.

"You don't have to take Boyd. Not unless you're snooping around."

I wrinkled my nose. "Snooping is such an unattractive word. It makes me think of the nosy neighbors peeking out their windows."

He put his arms around my waist and smiled. "Your snooping is attractive. Or at least, you look attractive while you're snooping."

I rolled my eyes, and my hands found their way into the back of his hair. "Can't we call it something else?"

"Like what?" he asked, kissing my forehead.

Every coherent thought left my head. Our relationship was definitely changing, but I felt like I needed someone to tell me the rules. If he could come up and kiss my head, did that mean I could walk up and kiss his jaw? I wasn't sure why I'd always wanted to do that. What about hand holding? And what about in public? And kissing. Did that only happen under special circumstances, and who should say when? This was why I didn't date much.

We hadn't ever been on a date. That seemed like an important step that shouldn't be skipped. Did Jett even want to date me? Maybe the mistletoe had just made everything a little weird. We wouldn't be standing here like this if that hadn't happened.

"Can't we call it sleuthing or something?" I asked when I realized I hadn't answered.

He grinned. "Sleuthing? I guess that word fits you occasionally, but snooping fits every time."

"Ha ha."

The door opened, and snow blew into the entryway. Eric walked in. Snow covered his hair and coat. I tried to step away from Jett without looking like I'd done anything wrong.

"It's cold out there," Eric said. "I shoveled the driveway in case we're able to get out, but I don't see it happening today. I've never seen snow like this."

Jett looked out at the snow. "You shoveled the driveway? That thing is massive."

Eric grinned. "When I say shoveled, I mean I got on a riding snowblower."

Jett chuckled. "I see."

"I don't get to do many fun jobs at this place, but that one's my favorite." He closed the door and took off his boots.

"I need to get back to the kitchen. Can someone let the others know breakfast will still be at seven o'clock?" I said.

"I'll let them know," Eric said.

I walked back to the kitchen with Jett a few steps behind me. José had breakfast well underway, and Anton and Boyd had joined him.

"What can I do?" I asked.

"Cookies?" José suggested.

"I thought they didn't want cookies?"

"That was Silvia. She said cookies aren't fancy enough. I doubt anyone will complain. Some people might need some comfort food today."

I nodded and went to the mixer. I can make cookies without thinking. I'd done it so many times.

"Where did you put Silvia's body?" Boyd asked. "I don't want to run into it anywhere."

Jett sighed. "We lost it."

"Lost it?"

"Someone took it."

Anton's eyes went wide. "This is all a little much. I wish we weren't stuck here."

"I'm going to walk around the outside," Jett said. "I need to clear my head."

"I bet." Boyd grinned. "It looks like Ivy's been messing with your hair again."

Boyd could be such a punk. José and Anton were smiling, and Jett ran his hands through his messy hair.

"How many cookies should I make?" There was no point in asking since I always made the same amount, but I didn't need any more teasing.

"A few dozen?" José suggested.

I pulled out the butter and sighed. There were so many other things I wanted to do right now.

I walked around the area where I'd seen Silvia's body. There had to be a clue somewhere. I walked to the side of the stairs. A closet door against the stairway caught my eye. We hadn't noticed it last night in the dark. It would be the perfect place to stash something quickly.

A chill went up my spine as I placed my hand on the doorknob. I felt ninety percent sure Silvia's body was going to fall out. Getting Jett was probably the smart thing to do, but there was the ten percent chance I was wrong, and I didn't want to drag him away from what he was doing.

I turned the doorknob and slowly opened it. Relief flooded me when no body fell onto me. I frowned as I peered in. It wasn't a closet. It was a passage. I shut the door and scurried through the house and into the kitchen. Jett wasn't there.

"There's a secret passage under the stairs!" I blurted out. "That has to be how someone took the body. Where's Jett?"

"I don't know," José said, "but don't go in there until you find him."

"I'll go with you," Boyd said.

"I don't know what's wrong with all you people," Anton complained from his place at the stove. "It's like you're always trying to put yourselves in dangerous situations."

"We don't try to," Ivy said. "It just happens."

"But you all chase it. I don't want anything to do with it. I'll just keep cooking and minding my business."

"We can't cook all day," I said. "I'm going to look for Jett."

The house felt empty. Everyone had come down for breakfast, then gone back to their rooms. Jett could be anywhere. I returned to where Silvia had died and went up the stairs. This house didn't make a lot of sense. This floor was considered the third floor even though it was only a floor above the main floor. The second floor was up a different staircase on the other side of the house and was lower than the third floor. I couldn't wrap my head around it.

Everything was quiet here, so I went to the second-floor area of the house. I walked quietly down the hallway until I heard voices behind a door. I pressed my ear to the door and listened.

"It's not your fault," Eric said.

"How can you say that?" a woman said. "It's completely my fault!"

"No. If your aunt was reasonable, you wouldn't have done it."

I frowned. He must be talking to Amanda or Jennifer.

"If I hadn't done it, this probably wouldn't have happened! The sheriff is asking a lot of questions. He's going to figure it out."

"No. I'm telling you, you aren't to blame."

"I'm going to spend the rest of my life in prison."

"No, they're going to straighten it all out, and your life will improve. You'll get the money Zeb wanted you to have, and your aunt won't be ruling your every move anymore."

I knocked on the door, and it went quiet. I heard someone walk across the wooden floor, and the door opened a crack. A woman with messy reddish-brown hair poked her head out. I think it was Jennifer, but I wasn't positive.

"Yes?" she said.

I gave her a sympathetic smile. Her eyes were red and puffy.

"I was just wondering if there is anything I can do for you?"

"Oh. No, thank you."

"Can I bring you some hot chocolate or a cookie?"

Her eyes brightened up slightly. "That would be nice."

"I'll be right back." She closed the door, and I hurried off to the kitchen. I'd give Eric time to leave so they wouldn't know I knew they were together.

Jett was in the kitchen talking to José. I grabbed a plate and piled it with cookies. We had the hot chocolate maker going so Jett could get some when he came in from looking outside. I poured some into a mug.

"What are you doing?" Jett asked.

"I'm taking this to Jennifer. I think she needs it."

"José said you found a secret passage."

"I don't know if it's a secret, but I did find a passage."

"I'm going to check it out."

I frowned. I wanted to go with him, but I needed to take this to Jennifer. We walked out of the kitchen together, and I stepped close to him. "I heard Jennifer and Eric talking. Could Silvia's death have been an accident?"

He frowned. "I doubt it."

"From what I heard, Jennifer sounded like she was confessing."

"She said she did it?"

"No, but it almost sounded like she confessed to causing an accident. I'm going to try to talk to her."

Jett nodded. "I'm going to the passage."

"You should wait for me."

"We can cover more if we split up."

I scowled. "But if you go by yourself and need backup, that's not ideal."

He grinned. "I won't need backup. I've got this."

I wasn't convinced, but I made my way to Jennifer's room. When she opened the door, she looked better than five minutes ago. She'd brushed her hair, and she smiled.

"Come in," she said. "You can put that on the table in the corner." I obeyed. It felt weird. It would make more sense for her to take the treats from me and walk to the table herself, but maybe that wasn't how the Clementses worked.

I set the plate and mug on the table, and she sat down. "Let me know if I can help with anything. I'm sorry you have to go through this."

"Thanks. Do you want to sit?"

I blinked in surprise. Jennifer must not be like her aunt. Silvia didn't seem the type to sit with the help. I sat down and watched her bite into a cookie.

"That's really good," she said. "I haven't had a cookie in ages. My aunt Silvia was against cookies. She was against most desserts, actually. She only had you make cinnamon rolls because one of her guests likes them so much."

"I eat too many desserts," I admitted.

Jennifer took a sip of hot chocolate. "I probably would if Silvia let me."

I raised my brows. Jennifer was about forty. I couldn't imagine allowing one of my relatives to dictate what I could eat. My aunt Linda had bossed me around when I first came to Muddy Creek, but only about the diner.

"This is a nice house. It must have been fun to grow up here."

"I suppose. I always wished we lived in town. It's a little secluded out here."

"Did you go to Muddy Creek for school?"

She laughed bitterly. "No. We had a tutor, and we're homeschooled."

"Oh, I see." I didn't want to stop talking since Jennifer seemed in the mood to chat. "I always wished I was home-schooled."

Jennifer took another sip. "It might work for some people, but it made us too secluded. My parents didn't want to homeschool us, but Aunt Silvia thought it was necessary. It's probably the reason we're all screwed up."

I was a little surprised that Jennifer was being so open, but then I saw an empty liquor bottle on her green bed-spread. I hoped she hadn't been the one to drink the entire thing, and I especially hoped she hadn't drunk it all since yesterday. She didn't seem too tipsy.

"What will you do now?" I asked.

"Who knows? I don't know who all Silvia's money will go to. Probably Kyle. I just hope Uncle Clint doesn't get it. He's not even a true Clements. He only married Silvia for her money."

"How do you know?"

"Why else would anyone marry her? I'm surprised he hasn't drunk himself to death."

I pointed at the empty bottle. "I hope no one does."

She waved her hand in dismissal. "There was barely a third of a bottle when I took that."

"Will you keep living here?"

She sighed. "Probably. Grandpa Zeb's will said we could all stay here until we die. I'm sure I'll die here, unmarried and forgotten."

I didn't know what to say to that.

Jennifer yawned. "My parents aren't nearly as strict and bossy as Silvia. Maybe I'll start dating. You hear that, Silvia's ghost? I'm going to date, and it will be someone you don't approve of!"

I pressed my lips together. "Silvia didn't let you date?"

"Silvia doesn't let anyone do anything. She had control of all the money, so she was the boss. I would have gotten married years ago if it wasn't for her."

"Is that the same for Kyle?"

She laughed. "No. Kyle won't ever get married. He's a jerk. He makes all the maids think he's ready to run off with them, then breaks their hearts and moves on to the next. He's got both Maria and Callie convinced he loves them. It's pathetic. That's been his way since he was eighteen."

"And Silvia was okay with that?"

"She pretended she didn't know. She was good at being delusional." Jennifer sipped her hot chocolate and swayed slightly. She was drunk, and she was just good at not showing it. The fact that she was dumping this all out on a stranger was probably another sign.

"Who do you think killed Silvia?" I asked.

She frowned, and tears began rolling down her face. "I don't know. I bet it was an accident." She stood and walked to her bed. She tossed the bottle to the floor and crawled under her comforter. I took that as my sign to leave.

Chapter 9

I watched Maria scrub the stove and waited an hour for Jett to turn up. I felt anxious and bored. When he didn't show, I got Boyd, and we went to the passage. I opened the door, and we peeked in. The passage was clean, which made me think it was well-used. It was only the size of a door, so Boyd had to walk behind me. There were lights inside, so we didn't need the flashlights we brought.

The walls were dark brown brick, just like the outside of the house. The floor was covered in grayish-brown carpet. It wasn't as exciting as I would have hoped a passage would be. The carpet had lines from a vacuum, but some tracks showed more than one person had walked around since it was last cleaned.

"This is interesting," Boyd said. "Who carpets their secret passage?"

"They must use it for something." The passage divided, and we turned to the right. "I wonder if it goes throughout the entire house."

"Probably," he said. "It's probably a good way for servants to get around without being seen. Do you have any theories yet?"

I shrugged. "I'm not sure. Jennifer's behind something, but I'm not completely sure what. Whatever it was sounds like it might have been an accident."

"Who's Jennifer again?"

"Silvia's niece. She's one of Lionel Clements's daughters."

"Right," Boyd said. "She's the one who sneaks around with the butler."

I stopped and turned to look at him. "What do you mean?"

"I saw the two of them smooching in the corner yesterday."

"Hmm. I heard them talking earlier. He was telling her something wasn't her fault. She's feeling guilty about something."

"Probably guilty about dating a murderer."

"We don't know who the murderer is."

"It has to be Eric. I'm telling you, the butler is always the one you should check first. Especially the butler who's secretly dating the bossy rich lady's niece."

"It's kind of funny the Clements children are all in their forties and falling for the staff. Jennifer said they're never allowed to do things, so I'm guessing the staff are the only people they socialize with. I can't see how money would be worth following Silvia's rules."

"People do weird things for money."

We turned past a few doors, but I assumed they went back into the house. I wanted to stay in the passage. We turned another corner, and I stopped and gasped. Jett was on the floor, lying on his stomach. I ran to his side and dropped to my knees.

"Jett?" I said, shaking his shoulder. "Jett?"

"Is he...?" Boyd started.

"He's breathing," I said.

He moaned and pushed himself up with his arms. "Ivy?" He sat up and held his head.

"Are you hurt?" I asked.

He touched the back of his head and flinched. "Someone hit me. I heard them run off, but I wasn't seeing straight."

"I told you not to come here alone," I scolded.

"Yeah, but I don't work for you."

I frowned.

"Don't take that the wrong way."

I stood and held out my hand. He took it, and I helped pull him up. He grabbed his head and swayed. I put my arms around him to help steady him. "I'm alright. I need to go lie down."

"What happened?" Boyd asked.

"No clue. I've been walking all over these passages. I thought I heard something behind me, and the next thing I knew, I opened my eyes and saw you two. I don't think I was actually knocked out, though. Just a bit dazed."

"Let's get you to your room," I said, keeping my arm around his waist. He draped his arm over my shoulders, and we began walking back the way we'd come. I didn't think he really needed my support, but it felt nice to pretend to be useful.

I paused in front of a door. All the other doors were dark wood, but this one was a little shorter and lighter in color. "This door is different," I said, moving away from Jett. I tried to open it, but it was locked.

Jett reached into his pocket and pulled out his wallet. "That's not a very good lock. We can probably pop it with a credit card." He pulled one from his wallet and handed it to me. I stuck it between the door and the lock, and it easily opened.

I pulled open the door, and we all stared inside. It was a closet. There was a mop bucket and other cleaning supplies, and Silvia's body was on the floor.

"Well, that solves one mystery," Boyd said.

"Now what?" I asked.

Jett's mouth turned down. "I can't move her. I'm still dizzy. I don't want to leave it here, though. We can't have it disappearing again."

"I'll go get José and Anton," I said. "You two can stand here and guard it. We need to find a weapon to leave with you."

Jett touched his side. "I have a gun."

"You do?" I asked. "I've never seen it."

"I almost always have it. I don't flash it around. I'm not sure you should be running around without anything."

I pulled my pepper spray from my pocket. "I'll keep this in my hand." I turned and ran through the passage before anyone could protest. It was good I'd paid attention to the way we'd come. I burst out of the door under the stairs and stopped when I saw Eric halfway up the stairs.

He raised his brows. "That's an odd place for you to be."

"I can't believe there are actual secret passages."

Eric grinned. "Passages, but not secret. Everyone who lives here knows about them. It makes it easier to get around when there's a party or to stay out of sight if you work here."

I wasn't sure if Eric could be trusted, but I needed a legit-sounding reason for being in there. "I thought Silvia's body might be in there," I said.

He frowned. "Was it?"

"No—Well, to be honest, I didn't go very far. I thought it was a secret area, but the more I thought about it, the more it looked like a place that gets used. I mean, it has carpet."

"Yes, the carpet keeps things quiet when the staff moves around in there. When we are fully staffed, we have thirty employees."

"Wow. I'm surprised they give so many of them time off together."

"Yes, it's always been their way. I think the Clementses like to take a break from so many people in the house. Of course, not all of us get it off."

"I'm sorry you don't."

"It's fine. I get time off in the summer."

I wanted to hurry to the kitchen, but I didn't want Eric to know I was going for help. I wasn't sure how I felt about him. He seemed like a nice guy, but his conversation with Jennifer made him appear a little suspicious. He could be hiding things for her.

"I spent some time talking to Jennifer. She seems nice."

"She is. Jennifer and Amanda aren't like the other Clementses. The way Silvia treated her family borders on criminal. She had a say in everything, or she would stop giving them money. I hope this allows Jennifer and Amanda a chance to lead normal lives."

"No one seems too distressed about Silvia's death."

He shrugged. "It's not surprising. I dated one of the Clements girls for a while. Silvia found out and put an end to it. It's made things a bit awkward for me."

"I bet. But you stayed."

"They pay well. It can be a bad idea to date someone you'll have to see all the time if it doesn't work out." He gave me a pointed look, and I frowned. Was he talking about me and Jett? He had come in the time we were hugging in the hall.

"I guess."

"Are you and the sheriff a thing?"

I took a deep breath. "I don't know what we are."

He nodded. "I've been there. Good luck."

"Thanks."

I hurried to the kitchen and found José and Anton. "Hey, guys. Someone hit Jett in the head Jett in the passage, and we found Silvia's body."

José frowned. "Is he okay?"

"Yeah, but he's dizzy. We need to get Silvia's body out of there, so he's guarding it with Boyd."

Anton shivered. "I don't want to be part of this. I know I'm a wimp, but this stuff is not my thing."

"Fine, José and I will move the body."

Anton frowned. "Do you not see how creepy that sounded?"

José followed me to the passage. Eric was gone, so we went in. We hurried to the place where Jett and Boyd stood guard.

Jett was crouched in the closet, examining Silvia. "Now that it's light, I'm almost positive she was stabbed. I'm not a professional about things like this, but that's my guess.

"Have you searched all the bedrooms?" I asked.

"No. I've searched everything else. Lionel Clements has been cooperative. I assume he's in charge here now that his sister's gone, but it might be Clint. He said I could go anywhere, but I thought I would wait to do the rooms people are staying in. I ran through all of them but didn't have time to be thorough."

"Aren't they more likely to have clues?"

"Possibly. If I were the killer, I would try to get any evidence as far away from me as I could. Where's Anton?"

"He won't come."

"Alright. José and I can move her."

"I can help. You're hurt."

"You go back with Boyd. I'm feeling better. I'm going to try to get the body to my truck. I'll lock it inside, and I don't think anyone would think to look in there."

I nodded. I didn't really want to carry a body. Boyd and I went back to the kitchen. We didn't need to spend a lot of time in the kitchen, but we didn't know where else to congregate. Kyle Clements was sitting at the island eating a cookie.

"Good cookies," he said when we entered.

"Thanks," I said. "I'm sorry about your mom."

He shrugged. "These things happen."

"It must be hard."

"You wouldn't say that if you knew her." He grabbed another cookie. "I'm eating as many cookies as I can in case she comes back to life and stops me."

Anton raised his eyebrow and pretended to be cooking. There wasn't a lot for us to do.

"She was against cookies?"

"She was against everything."

"That's too bad."

"Yeah, well, now we can all live our lives. I'm not wasting any more time on her."

"I guess the house is yours now?" Boyd asked.

"No idea. There's a lot of speculation about that. My grandpa's will was tampered with. Everyone knows it, and everyone knows my mom did it, but no one can prove it. Unless we find the real one, who knows what will happen?"

"Why would she tamper with it?"

He pushed his brown hair from his eyes. "She could have a million reasons. She loved to be in control of everything, and I'm sure my grandpa wouldn't have left everything to her like he did."

"Why not?"

He grabbed another cookie. "They clashed pretty badly. Grandpa got along with my uncle Lionel better than my mom. If he was going to leave the majority of his wealth to someone, it would be Lionel, not her. We all know it, but no one can prove it."

The door opened, and Maria poked her head in and looked at Kyle.

"Excuse me, will you?" Kyle asked. He went out the door, and I took a deep breath. I wanted to hear what they were going to say. Tiptoeing to the door, I tried to listen. I could hear them walking away. I quietly opened the door and watched them go around a corner. Pursing my lips, I followed them. I could hear them talking, so I pressed myself against the wall and listened. I needed to be silent since they were only around the corner.

"What's stopping you now?" Maria said. "She's gone. There's nothing to keep us apart."

"Come on, Maria. She just died. I can't go running off with you right now. I need to deal with things so I don't end up with nothing."

"We don't need anything."

He chuckled. "You can't live on nothing. There's a good chance I could come out really well if I play my cards right."

"I'll wait, but not long."

"You know I'm worth it," he teased.

I could hear them kissing, and I felt like a creep. I moved silently away and back to the kitchen.

"We need to get out of this place," Anton said.

I frowned. "The snow is still coming down hard. I can't even see the tires on Jett's truck."

"Might as well get comfy," Boyd said from his place at the island.

"Has anyone checked on the Clementses' guests?" I asked. I'd seen them briefly, but they were sticking to their room as far as I knew.

"Nope," Boyd said. "I bet they're staying out of sight."

"What if they did it?"

"It's possible."

"There's something about Kyle Clements that I don't trust," I said. "He's in the hall right now kissing Maria."

"What?" Callie exclaimed, rushing in from the back entrance. "Where are they?"

My eyes widened. "Oh, umm..."

Callie tore out of the kitchen, her blond ponytail swinging behind her. I grimaced. "This might not go well."

A minute later, we heard yelling. I rushed down the hall to see Maria and Callie hitting each other. Maria threw Callie to the floor and jumped on her. Kyle stood against the wall, chewing his gum and watching.

"Stop them!" I commanded.

Kyle shrugged. "What good will that do? We're all stuck here together. They'll just find each other again."

"This is all your fault," I said as Maria punched Callie in the face.

Kyle shrugged.

I grabbed Maria and pulled her off Callie. Her hand flew back and caught me in the eye. I threw her to the side. Callie was no match for Maria. She sat on the floor crying and holding her fat lip.

Maria stood and charged forward. I put my hand up, and she crashed into it. My wrist throbbed, but I ignored it.

"Stop!" I yelled. "This is stupid! You realize what you're doing, right? You're attacking the wrong person!"

Maria took several deep breaths, and Callie wiped her eyes.

"If you want to punch someone, it should be him." I pointed at Kyle. "He's the lying scumbag."

Kyle just chewed his gum and stared at me.

"Look, he doesn't care about either of you."

Maria's eyes narrowed, and she charged him. Kyle's eyes widened as her fist collided with his eye.

"Ouch!" he yelled, pushing her to the floor.

"I hate you!" Maria said from the ground.

"Who cares?" he said. "You're a maid. You really think I'm going to spend my life with a maid? Both of you are delusional. Just like every other maid who's ever worked here." He chuckled.

Clint came around the corner. "What is everyone yelling about?"

"Your son is a lying dog!" Callie said from the floor. I held out my hand and helped her to her feet.

Clint sighed and looked at Kyle. "He's his own man."
He walked past them without another look.

Kyle sneered. "You two are both fired."

Maria's eye twitched.

"As soon as this storm clears up, I never want to see you again."

Callie ran down the hall and disappeared, and Maria stomped after her. I glared at Kyle.

"What?" he asked. "Every maid who has ever lived should know that the handsome, rich bachelor will only fall for a maid if it's in a movie. It serves them right for being stupid."

"It's no wonder your family keeps to themselves," I said, turning and walking away. When I got to the kitchen, Jett and José were back.

"Girl fight in the hall?" Boyd asked.

"Yes."

"What happened to your eye?" Jett asked.

I ignored the throbbing and smiled. "I broke the fight up."

"We need to stop talking in the kitchen. It's too easy for people to overhear," Boyd said.

I nodded. "So where do we go?"

"Jett's room is the farthest from everything," José said.

Anton sat in the corner reading a book. He looked up. "I'm staying right here so everyone knows I'm not a part of any of this."

Chapter 10

I sat next to Jett at the foot of his bed, and José and Boyd sat on chairs they'd pulled over from a small table. I told them all the conversations I'd overheard and everyone I'd talked to. Jett told us he and José had gotten Silvia's body to his truck and locked it after covering it with a blanket.

"Now what?" Boyd asked.

Jett rubbed his eyes. "I need to search everyone's rooms."

"Start with the butler."

Jett shook his head. "I think Jennifer sounds guilty."

"But she was saying something about an accident," I said. "You can't accidentally stab someone and throw them down the stairs."

"What if she was trying to kill someone else?" José asked.

"Have you talked to the two guests?" I asked Jett.

He rubbed the sore spot on the back of his head. "Their names are Merv and Kellie Griffin. I don't think they're involved. They seem pretty terrified. I'll be surprised if they leave their room for anything but meals. They hadn't even wanted to come, but they were afraid of offending Silvia."

"What about Lionel's wife?" I asked. "I can't think of who she is."

"She's not here. She had a business meeting in Wichita."

"I'm leaning toward Kyle," José said. "He sounds like a real jerk."

I moved my lips to the side. "Hmm. Maybe. He's definitely a jerk, but what would his motive be?"

"Get his mom's money."

"I thought that at first, but that would just be so he could marry Maria or whatever. Now that we know he wasn't serious about her, I don't see the point. Silvia probably gave him plenty of money."

"I don't get all these people in their forties living like sheltered kids," Boyd said. "They all need to take control of their lives."

"Not having money must scare them," I said. "Should we show the family the will?" I said, holding up my phone.

"I don't think so," Jett said. "Not until we know more. I think we can safely say Silvia altered the will. My question is, did Clint and Kyle know? They would benefit from her getting the biggest share. If they knew, they probably didn't kill her."

"It was the butler," Boyd said again.

I smiled. "You can't just blame the butler because of something you saw on TV. What would his motive be?"

"You said he dated one of the Clementses. Maybe he could date her again with Silvia out of the way."

"Has anyone talked to Amanda?"

"Who?" José asked.

"Jennifer's sister."

"I talked to her," Jett said. "She wouldn't say much, just that everyone probably has a motive since Silvia wasn't the nicest person."

"Jett looks like trash," Boyd said. "We should leave and let him get some rest."

Jett yawned. "Gee, thanks, Boyd."

"We could all use some sleep," José said. "We're not going to do anyone any good if we never sleep."

José and Boyd stood. "Are you alright?" I asked Jett. "What if you have a concussion or something?"

"I'm fine. I want all of you to lock your doors."

"You lock yours too," I said.

"I always lock my door. I even lock my door when I'm in the bathroom and no one else is in my house."

Boyd laughed. "That borders on paranoid."

Jett smiled. "Good night."

"Night," Boyd said. José tossed a wave over his shoulder as he left the room with Boyd.

I looked at my phone. "It's only seven thirty."

Jett shrugged. "It's been a long couple of days."

"Let me look at your head."

He rubbed the spot. "It's fine. Just a little bump. It probably looks better than your eye."

I touched my eye. It was sensitive to the touch, but I hadn't felt it since a few minutes after it happened.

"Let me look at your head."

He rolled his eyes. "If it makes you happy."

I crawled behind him and got on my knees, then began carefully moving his hair.

"It's here," he said, pointing.

"I feel like a monkey searching for bugs." I moved the hair and saw a small purple bump. "Hmm. It's hardly anything."

"That's what I said."

"But it knocked you out. You must be sensitive."

"Ha ha. I wasn't knocked out, just dazed."

I put my arms around his neck, going against my inse-curities. I pressed my cheek to his. "Just be careful, alright? Being the sheriff doesn't make you invincible."

"I know." He grabbed my hands and stood, pulling me onto his back.

I squealed. "Put me down!"

"Nope. I'm taking you to your room, and I want you to stay in there until tomorrow." He opened the door and walked into the hall.

"What if someone sees?" I said quietly, not to draw attention.

"I think you're the one who put yourself there."

"Your head's hurt. Don't make it worse."

"It's fine."

"Piggyback rides are for three-year-olds."

"Sometimes it's good to be a kid again." He released my hands when we got to my door, and I slid to my feet.

"I can't believe you did that."

He grinned. "Sure you can. Now, go inside and lock the door."

"Thank you."

"For what?"

"I don't know." I went on my toes and kissed his jaw. Finally. Turning around, I slipped into my room and closed the door, locking it. My steps echoed across the floor, and I jumped onto my bed. I lay there staring at the ceiling and smiled.

I'd had plenty of crushes in my day, but this was the first time I'd felt like this. Jett made my heart crazy. This was what all the songs on the radio were about. I put my hand to my heart and counted the beats. It was going fast. I couldn't believe it had taken me twenty-nine years to have this feeling.

He might have kissed me if I'd paused for a moment, but that had taken all of my courage. I had to run away and pull myself back together. A minute later, there was a soft knock on the door. I walked over and opened it a crack. It was Jett.

"Is something wrong?" I asked.

He arched his eyebrow. "Yes, something is wrong." He grabbed my hand and pulled me back into the hall. "Don't think you can do that, then just run away."

"What are you talking about?" I asked.

He wrapped his arms around my waist. "You know what." He leaned down and pressed his warm lips to mine. My hands gripped his shoulders, and I made a conscious effort to keep my hands from his sore head.

"Hey! I thought you told us all to go to bed," Boyd said. "My word. If I had known what the two of you would be like, I never would have been so encouraging."

I reluctantly pulled away from Jett. Jett chuckled and kissed my cheek. "Don't let Boyd embarrass you. He doesn't have to look." He leaned down and kissed me again.

"Alright, come on," Boyd said. "I'll make sure the sheriff gets locked into his room."

I smiled. "Thanks, Boyd."

"Sure thing."

A loud explosion caused me to pop up from my bed. The sun shone through the cracks of the curtains, so it had to be morning. I hurried to the window and looked out. Jett's truck was on fire. From what I could see, it didn't look salvageable. I grabbed my robe and pulled it on, then ran through the house to the front door.

The door was open, and Eric stood in the doorway. His arms were crossed over his chest against the bitter cold. I grabbed my boots and pulled them on. I moved past Eric and saw Jett walking around his truck.

José stood off to the side, watching the truck burn. I could hear others behind me coming outside to see what was happening.

I rushed over to Jett. "Shouldn't we try to put it out?"

He placed his arm over my shoulders. "No. It's gone. It's too cold to use the hose, and we still can't call anyone."

"I'm sorry."

"The truck's not the problem. Silvia's body was in there."

"Right."

"I'm probably going to get fired. I've screwed this entire thing up."

I put my arm around him. "That's not true."

He sighed and pulled me closer.

"What happened?" Lionel asked.

"Someone was trying to destroy evidence," Jett said, not bothering to release me.

"What evidence?"

"We found Silvia's body. We put it in the truck to keep it safe."

"I'd call that a failure," Lionel said.

Jett nodded.

"We just have to let it burn itself out," Kyle said. "It should be alright with the snow all around."

"I'll stay out and make sure no rogue flames catch anything else on fire," José offered. "Breakfast is ready and on the table."

"Come join us," Lionel said. "All of you." Everyone from the house was outside. I wondered if he really meant everyone. It turned out he did. He even had Eric, Maria, and Callie at the table. I couldn't imagine Silvia would have ever done this.

We all sat quietly at the table, eating José's pancakes. Callie kept shooting dirty looks at Kyle, but he only smiled. Maria sat next to me. Her cheeks were pink, and she looked cold and tired. She also smelled like gasoline. I would have to tell Jett. Clint wasn't eating pancakes. He just took an occasional drink from his bottle.

Eric looked uncomfortable. He'd been working here for years and had probably never sat down with the family. He sat with Jennifer on one side and Amanda on the other. The Griffins looked like they would rather be anywhere but here.

I tried eating my pancakes, but they felt too thick to swallow. Maria had to have been the one to blow up the truck. Why else would she smell like gas? She might also have been the one to kill Silvia. She had been the one to find her first, and she'd had reason to want Silvia out of the way.

"We were told there was a lot of security when we came," I said. "Are there cameras?"

"No cameras," Lionel said. "Silvia was worried people would use cameras against us. She was paranoid about things like that."

"She should have had indoor cameras," Clint said. "Then we would know which one of you killed her to get our money."

Lionel's eyes narrowed. "Your money? That money all came from our family. You aren't entitled to any of it."

"I am, as Silvia's husband."

Lionel slammed his fist into the table. "Everyone here knows Silvia changed the will. Maybe you helped her."

"Please," Clint scoffed. "Why would I do that?"

"For the same reasons you married Silvia. The money. You'll never convince me you married Silvia because you were in love with her. You two have never gotten along. I bet you killed her."

"I didn't kill her! That was probably you. You're jealous her father left her most of his money."

"You know he didn't."

I opened my mouth to speak, but Jett shook his head so I clamped it shut.

Jett stood. "There was a different will." Everyone stopped and looked at him. "Someone bought Zeb's wardrobe. It had a false bottom. The will was in the bottom."

Clint folded his arms. "So where is it?"

"Unfortunately, the woman who found it mailed it back to this house. I don't know which of you must have it. It might have been Silvia. Does anyone want to confess?"

Everyone looked suspiciously at one another.

"Without the will, nothing changes," Clint said.

Jet shook his head. "Thankfully, there was a picture taken of the will. We can deal with all of it once we're no longer stuck here."

"Who knows about this will?" Kyle asked. "Just the people here?"

I rolled my eyes. Did Kyle think he could take us all out to hide information about the will?

"No, there are several people." Jett was lying. The only other person who knew was Barbra. "It's already being investigated."

Clint and Kyle frowned, and Maria looked like she might burst into tears.

"What did it say?" Amanda asked.

"The money was supposed to be divided between Lionel, Silvia, Amanda, Jennifer, and Kyle equally."

"I knew it," Lionel muttered. "Silvia's lucky she's dead."

Kyle stood and marched over to his uncle. Jett rushed over to them and caught Kyle's arm when he tried to throw a punch. He grabbed Kyle and dragged him back to his spot, and threw him into his chair. I tried not to look too impressed.

"Everyone stay in your seats," Jett growled.

"How dare you touch me!" Kyle said, straightening his shirt.

Jett pointed at him. "Don't speak."

Kyle crossed his arms and glared.

"Things aren't going well, if you haven't noticed. If anyone wants to confess before it gets worse, now is your chance."

Everyone sat staring at him.

"Fine. We'll do it the hard way. Are there any big tarps? We're going to need one to put over the truck and Silvia."

"Why?" Kyle asked.

Jett rolled his eyes. "To protect any evidence."

Lionel rubbed his chin. "I think we have some in the garage."

"Great. I'm going to search everyone's rooms. Does anyone object?"

"You can't search through our personal things," Maria said.

"You were fired," Kyle said. "You don't have a room anymore. We just haven't kicked you out because of the storm."

"You can't fire Maria!" Amanda said. "She's not replaceable."

Kyle glared at his cousin. "She's fired. So's Callie."

"Why?" Jennifer asked.

"I don't have to answer to you."

"I'm so sick of you," Amanda said. "You've been a self-centered jerk since high school. Once the will is figured out, I'm out of here."

"You can't leave," Lionel said. "The Clementses live here. That's the way it is."

"We've missed so much of our life!" Amanda said. "First, Grandpa Zeb bossed us around, then Aunt Silvia. I'm not going to stay around and have my life dictated by anyone else."

"I agree," Jennifer said. "Who cares about money when our entire life is ruled by someone else?"

"They have a point," Kyle said.

"Be quiet, Kyle," Jennifer said. "You've been allowed to do a lot more than we have, and you still turned out horrid."

"What did I get that you didn't?"

"You were able to go to college and come and go as you please."

"You could have left."

"That's enough!" Lionel said. "Everyone stop before you ruin all family relationships."

"I don't care about any relationship except with Amanda," Jennifer said.

"This can all be worked out later," Jett said. "Right now, we need to figure out who killed Silvia."

"Where's Maria?" I asked.

"Great. She's probably burning all my things," Kyle said. "We shouldn't have given her a room with a fireplace. She's always burning things."

Jennifer shrugged. "It would serve you right."

Kyle began to stand, but Jett pushed him back down.

"Let me up. I need to go check my things."

"I'll find Maria, then I'll search your rooms. Anyone who leaves this room will be arrested. Do you understand?" No one responded. "Good. José, let me know if anyone leaves. I suggest you all eat and don't talk."

Chapter 11

Jett held my hand, and we walked to Maria's room.

"She smelled like gasoline," I said. Jett had surprised me by bringing me with him.

"She was also the one who found Silvia, and her room isn't the closest."

When we got to her room, the door was locked. Jett pounded on it, but no one answered, so he jiggled the handle. "Open the door!" he yelled. He turned to me. "This lock is better than some. I won't be able to pick it."

I pushed on it. "It doesn't seem too strong. Can you kick it down?"

His mouth turned down. "Maybe. I don't want to destroy anything I don't have to."

I pounded on the door again. "Maria!" I yelled.

Jett sighed. "Alright, stand back." He kicked the door, and I cringed as it cracked. He kicked it again, and the door flew open. We entered. The room was empty, but the fireplace was going. Jett walked up to a closed door and listened. "I think she's in the shower."

I nodded. "She's probably trying to get the smell off her." I looked around the room. It wasn't much smaller than the one I was staying in, and it had a large bed and nice paintings of trees on the walls.

Jett pounded on the bathroom door. "Maria!"

"One moment!" she yelled.

Jett stood back, and we waited. It took five minutes for Maria to come out. Her long black hair dripped all over her yellow T-shirt.

Maria frowned. "You broke my door."

"You left the dining room before I said you could."

She raised her brow. "And?"

"Why did you leave?"

"To take a shower."

"Where are the clothes you were wearing?" he asked.

She pointed at a hamper. "In there somewhere."

Jett grabbed the black dress on top and smelled it. "Where's the one that smelled like gasoline?"

"I don't know what you're talking about."

"Did you throw it in the fireplace?"

"I'm not an idiot," she said, then closed her mouth.

Jett's eyes scanned the room. He moved a few things around and looked under the bed. He went into the bathroom and rummaged around. "Aha."

I looked at Maria. She swallowed and closed her eyes. He came out holding a wet black dress.

"It was in the toilet."

I wrinkled my nose. "And you touched it?"

He shrugged.

Maria crossed her arms. "Fine. I blew up your truck."

"Why?" he asked.

"To get rid of Silvia's body, obviously."

Jett walked to the garbage can and pulled out an empty sack. He tossed the dress inside and tied it shut. He pulled a pair of handcuffs out, and Maria frowned.

"Wash your hands before you touch me," she said.

"I don't trust you. Turn around, please."

Maria looked around the room, then bolted out the broken door. Jett caught up to her and knocked her down. He pushed her face near the floor and sat on her while he cuffed her.

"Don't touch my face with your nasty hands!" she protested. He pulled her to her feet and dragged her to the dining area. Everyone stared with wide eyes.

"Is there somewhere I can keep her until we can leave?" he asked Lionel. "I don't want to have to keep her handcuffed."

"Umm..." Lionel looked thoughtful.

"Why is she handcuffed?" Kyle asked. "She didn't kill Silvia."

"Yes, I did," Maria said, staring blankly at him.

Eric raised his brows, and Jennifer sank back into her chair and covered her face with her hands.

"We might be able to get out," Anton said, looking out the window. "It hasn't snowed in a few hours."

Jett glared at Maria. "Maybe if we had my truck. I don't know if I trust Ivy's car to get through this."

"Not with me driving," I said.

"I have a big truck with snow tires and four-wheel drive," Lionel said. "You're welcome to take it."

"We wouldn't all fit," I protested.

"I'll take Maria and Ivy. Ivy can make sure Maria doesn't try anything while I'm driving."

I handed my keys to José. "You can bring my car when the roads get better."

Lionel went to find his keys, then he took us into his massive garage. There were several vehicles, and all of them were expensive.

"That's a nice truck," Jett said. "I'm a little nervous to drive it in this snow."

Lionel shrugged. "It's just a truck. I'm not sentimental about it."

We climbed in. Jett was in the driver's seat, then me, then Maria. Jett handcuffed her to the armrest. Jett pulled onto the plowed driveway, and we made our way to the road. No plows came over this way, so it was slow going.

"This truck is amazing," Jett said. "I can't believe it's getting through this."

"It's so slow."

"But we aren't getting stuck."

We drove in silence until we got to the town. Jett pulled up to the sheriff's office and came to get Maria. I followed as he took her inside. The sheriff's office had two holding cells, and he put her in one. She lay on the small bed and stared up at the ceiling.

"Do you need me for anything else?" I asked.

"No," Jett said. "You can go home and rest. It's been a crazy few days. I can drive you."

"No, I'm going to go get Creepers, then I'll walk home."

I walked over to the library and went inside. Brian sat at his desk resting his elbows on top, his hands covering his curly black hair. He was reading something.

"Hi, Brian."

He looked up and smiled. "Hey, Ivy. I'm glad you got back safely. This snow is crazy."

"It is. We had to borrow the Clementses' truck."

"Jett's couldn't get through the snow?"

"Jett's got blown up."

"What?"

Creepers must have heard me because he came out from wherever he was hiding and meowed at my feet. I bent down and picked him up and cuddled him by my cheek.

"We can't seem to do anything without something crazy happening."

He grinned. "No bodies, though, right?"

I frowned. "Silvia Clements was murdered."

"Dang. I was joking when I said that. What happened?"

"It looks like the maid did it. She blew up Jett's truck, too. We couldn't call anyone because we had no service."

"No one in Muddy Creek has service. The storm took out the tower and we can't contact anyone to come fix it until the storm's over. I don't think we could get anyone to come fix it anyway until the roads get plowed."

"That's too bad. I think Jett wanted to call the police in Wichita so he can get some forensics people to come."

"We've missed Jett. Deputy Ledford is a pill. He's been bossing everyone around and causing all sorts of problems."

"About what?"

"A lot of trees and a few poles were knocked over. He doesn't think it's acceptable that we don't go try to fix them. He can't grasp the concept that no one here knows how and the weather is too bad."

"I'm surprised you're even open. Has anyone come in?"

"No. I come anyway, just so I don't go crazy at home."

"Thanks for watching Creepers."

"I enjoyed it."

"I haven't had any good sleep since I left. I think I'll go take a quick nap."

"The diner's been closed almost since you left. Carrie was worried about everyone traveling through the snow."

I nodded. "That was smart. No one would come anyway, I'm sure. I'll talk to you later."

"Walk carefully."

"I will." I walked to the diner with Creepers meowing at me. He didn't like being out in the snow any more than I did. Luckily, it was close, and we made it before my toes froze. Creepers jumped from my arms as soon as we went in and ran up the stairs to our room. I followed and got him his food.

After taking a shower, I changed and sank into my warm bed. Creepers was probably confused, but he climbed onto the bed and curled up by my head. "I missed you," I told him. He rubbed his head against mine.

That was the last thing I remembered. When I woke up, it was dark. I shivered and rolled over. I sat up. Staring blankly ahead, I tried to think. "Oh no. We messed up." I hurried to change into my clothes and pulled on my boots and coat. I looked at the clock. It was 11:00. I couldn't go to Brian's at this time, so I was going to have to take Creepers with me. I grabbed his carrier and put him inside.

I walked through the dark, snowy town until I came to the sheriff's office. The lights were on, so I peeked in the glass door. Deputy Ledford was sleeping in a chair at the desk. He wasn't the one I needed to find.

I knew the street Jett lived on, but not which house. It was hard to get through the snow, and Creepers was not happy. I trudged down the street until I saw a house with a large willow tree. I remembered his mom told me it was the reason he got the house. I hoped this was the right one, or someone wouldn't be happy at this time of night.

Pounding on the door didn't do me any good. If Jett was here, he wasn't answering. It was freezing, and my fingers were getting stiff. I pounded again, then kicked the door a few times. After a minute, I heard someone fiddle with the lock. It opened, and Jett stood there in a blue robe, rubbing his eyes.

"Ivy, what are you doing? Is that Creepers?"

"Can I come in? I'm frozen."

He moved back, and I entered, putting the cat carrier on the floor.

"Do you have to do everything in the middle of the night?"

"We messed up," I said.

"What do you mean?" He closed the door, and I shivered.

"Come on," he said. "I'll get you some hot chocolate." I grabbed Creepers and followed him into a small tidy kitchen. I was impressed with how clean it was since he'd admitted to me once that he never made his bed. I sat at the small kitchen table.

He grabbed a mug and poured a packet of hot chocolate powder inside, then turned on the hot water. "What did we mess up?" he asked as he filled up the mug and stirred it. He put it in the microwave and turned to me.

"Maria couldn't have hit you in the passageway. I'd been watching her clean the stove before I went looking for you. I don't know if she killed Silvia, but she couldn't have gotten to you before I got there."

The microwave beeped, and Jett pulled out the mug. He stirred it again and handed it to me. "I knew something was off."

I sipped the hot chocolate. "That means we left our friends with a possible killer."

Jett sat across from me. "I don't think they're in danger. Whoever the killer is probably thinks they got away with it. They'll probably lie low and hope Maria really takes the fall." He rubbed his eyes. "Man. I wish you wouldn't have remembered it until morning."

"I probably should have waited. I'm sorry."

"No, it's fine. We should go in the morning. I don't want to get stranded in the dark."

"What about Maria?"

"I'm still pretty sure she blew up my car."

"I wonder if it was Kyle, and she was covering for him even though he treated her so poorly."

"That's the first thing that comes to my mind. We can talk to her in the morning before we head back. I don't want you walking back in the dark. I have a spare room you can use."

"Mmm, I don't know. Creepers usually sleeps all night but occasionally uses the litter box. I don't trust him not to go on the floor."

"I can put a box in there with wood shavings. If he goes on the floor, it's laminate, so it will clean easily."

"Alright." He led me to a small tan room with a twin bed covered in a blue blanket. The only other thing in the room was a nightstand.

"I'll be back," he said. I let Creepers out of the carrier, and he walked around, exploring the area. Jett came back with a small box full of shavings. He put it on the floor, and Creepers stepped in and batted the shavings around.

"I'm sorry I woke you."

"It's okay. I'll see you in the morning, alright?"

"Thanks. Good night."

"Night."

I flipped off the light and climbed into the bed. It wasn't overly comfortable, but it would do. I worried I wouldn't be able to sleep since I'd napped so long, but I quickly fell asleep with Creepers near my feet.

<h1 style="text-align:center">Chapter 12</h1>

The following morning, we woke up early and drove Lionel's truck to the sheriff's office. We stopped at Brian's house on the way and asked him to take Creepers again. When we got to the sheriff's office, Deputy Ledford frowned when we walked in. I had a feeling he hated me even though I gave him so much free dessert.

"Hey, Ledford," Jett said. "I need to talk to Maria." We walked back to the cell, and Ledford followed.

Maria sat on the bed reading a book. She looked up, and her mouth turned down.

"I know you didn't kill Silvia," Jett said.

Maria looked back at her book and didn't respond.

"Who are you covering for? It's not worth it."

"You don't understand," she said, turning the page.

"Tell me so I'll understand."

"No."

I grabbed the cell bars and looked in. "Kyle was a jerk to you. Why would you help him?"

She turned the page again and ignored me.

"Why do you always let her help you?" Ledford asked, pointing at me.

Jett glared at him and turned back to Maria. "Whenever you're ready to talk, let me know." We walked back into the office and shut the door to the prison area. Jett turned to Ledford. "I need to go back to the Clementses'. There are still some things I need to figure out."

Ledford crossed his arms. "And you're going to take her instead of me? That's not how this is supposed to work."

"I need you to take care of the town. I can't leave Ivy to do that. It needs to be someone who is trained."

Ledford puffed out his chest. "I suppose so. Still, I don't see why Miss Clark doesn't go back to her little diner and mind her business."

"I was at the Clementses' house catering for them, not trying to steal Jett from you." Saying it wasn't going to make him like me better, but it slipped out.

His eyes narrowed, but he didn't say anything.

Jett turned to me. "I'm going to run to Hal's shop. I think he has a satellite phone. Do you want to come?"

"No, if we might end up stuck at the Clementses' again, I want to grab a few things before we go."

"Alright. I'll meet you in front of the diner in twenty minutes."

He stepped forward and grabbed me in his arms, then kissed me right in front of Ledford. I was pretty sure he was doing it for Ledford's benefit, but I would enjoy it, anyway. When he pulled away, I couldn't help glancing at Ledford. He was crossing his arms and scowling.

"You know that isn't appropriate when you're on duty," he said.

Jett shrugged. "I'm technically still on vacation." He put his arm over my shoulders, and we left the building.

"You did that on purpose," I said.

He chuckled. "Maybe. That guy is on my last nerve. I don't know what he has against you."

"I think he's still mad I wouldn't give him all his food for free."

"Probably. It's good you didn't agree to it. He gets enough free desserts. If you gave him free meals, he'd be there three times a day."

The snow was so deep I had trouble getting my boot high enough to step. Most of the sidewalks were clear, but a few shops on the square hadn't shoveled yet this morning.

"Who clears the streets?" I asked. "I wouldn't think Muddy Creek would have a snow plow."

"Hal. He has a plow on his truck, and he made an agreement with the city. He gets paid, and we don't have to try to get someone to come from far away. No one wants to come this far unless they get paid a lot."

"Since you're going to talk to him anyway, could you ask him to plow up to the Clementses'? Then we wouldn't be stuck."

"I can ask." He gave me a squeeze, and we parted ways. I sighed as I felt more cold, and I hurried to the diner. I wondered how much money I would lose this week from the storms. There were only small flurries right now. I couldn't check to see what the weather was going to do since I had no internet.

Thirty minutes later, we were on our way back to the Clementses'.

"This truck is so nice," Jett said. "My truck would have been all over the place."

"How long will it take to get a new one?"

"I'm not sure."

"Did you own the truck?"

"No. It came with the job."

We drove in silence, and I tried to decide who I thought killed Silvia. If it wasn't Kyle, Maria must think it was. I still wasn't sure what to take from Jennifer and Eric's conversation. Jennifer definitely felt guilty about something.

"Whatcha thinking?" Jett asked.

"Maria must think Kyle's guilty. Do you?"

"She was mad at him. He fired her and had multiple girlfriends. Would she really try to make him look less guilty? She definitely blew up my truck. Why do that if she's not guilty?"

"I guess she could have killed Silvia but didn't hit you?"

He rubbed his chin and kept his eyes on the powdery road. "Who would attack me if they weren't guilty?"

"I don't know. Eric was just outside the passage. He doesn't seem the type, though. And why would he try to keep you from finding the body? He doesn't have a close connection to Maria. At least that I know about."

"I don't know. The people in that house seem to have all sorts of weird relationships going on."

"Maria seemed pretty crazy about Kyle, so I doubt she had anything going on with Eric. I guess she could be shallow. Kyle has a lot of money, but Eric's really attractive. Kyle has nothing on him when it comes to looks. Eric's also a lot more pleasant to talk to."

Jett side-eyed me. "Eric's all that, huh?"

I smiled. "It's pretty obvious, isn't it?"

He sighed. And stopped the truck and put it in park. "I thought I only had to compete with Brian, and that's hard enough."

I laughed. "Brian? What are you talking about?"

"You spend a lot of time with Brian. He's got a much better personality than me, and he's pretty good looking."

I stared at him and tried to gauge whether he was joking, but I couldn't tell. "I don't spend a lot of time with Brian."

"It feels like you do."

I tilted my head and studied him. "Are you serious? Brian's a good friend. He helps me with Creepers and book things, but that's all."

"Hmm. You sure?"

He looked like he was trying to make it into a joke, but I could tell he was serious. I suddenly remembered a few times Jett had seemed a little weird around Brian.

"You know he's way too old for me, right? He's in his forties. I count him as part of the old guy posse that helps me solve crimes."

"Okay, so let's talk about Eric. You like the butler? It's his suit, right?" He grinned, and his eyes sparkled.

"I don't like Eric. Saying he's attractive doesn't mean I like him. I'm just stating the obvious and looking for reasons for Silvia's murder."

"Alright. I'm done being insecure for the day."

I smiled. "I do have a big crush on someone."

"Oh?"

"I have a huge crush on the town sheriff."

"Yeah?"

"Yeah."

Jett grinned at me. "That's what I want to hear. Let's get moving." He put the truck in drive, and it went a few inches and stopped. He rocked it back and forth, but it didn't want to go. He backed up a few feet and went forward. "Whew. I thought we were stuck. I better not stop again. This truck really is amazing."

"Did you talk to Hal?"

"He said he might plow the road if he feels like it."

"That doesn't sound promising."

He laughed. "That's Hal's way. Easygoing and slow at everything. He gets to things when he gets to them. I offered him enough money to make it worth it, but I'm not sure he's bribeable."

"That's a good way to be. I'm totally bribeable."

"Oh yeah?"

"Give me chocolate with caramel, and I'm yours."

He chuckled. "I'll remember that."

"Oh no."

"What?"

I pointed to the side of the road, or what I assumed was the side of the road. For all I knew, we hadn't been anywhere near the road. There was no way to tell with this snow. My car sat there covered in snow.

"Someone must have tried to venture out. Don't worry. We'll dig it out," Jett said.

We turned into the Clementses' driveway and drove up the long path. "They didn't get very far."

"Nope. I bet they drove out of the driveway and were immediately stuck. A car can't take this snow."

It was faster going up the driveway than on the road because it was plowed. When we reached the house, José came rushing out in his big black coat.

I climbed out of the truck and smiled. I tried to ignore the lump in the snow that was Jett's truck and Silvia's body. "Hi, José. Are you the one who got my car stuck?"

He rolled his eyes. "That was Anton. He's not very patient. He promised to dig it out. That's the least of the problems around here."

Jett walked over. "Please tell me no one else is dead."

"No. It's just been crazy. Kyle and Callie got into a huge fight. Eric stood up for Callie, and Kyle tried to fire him. Lionel told Kyle if he didn't straighten up, he couldn't live here anymore."

Jett sighed. "I bet that went well."

"Kyle yelled at Lionel and told him he would probably end up owning the house and then he would kick him out."

"Did Kyle's father get involved?" I asked.

"Nah. Clint sat in the corner drinking. That guy needs help."

"Anything else?" Jett asked.

José shrugged. "That was the biggest thing. I caught Eric and Jennifer kissing. That was awkward."

"The Clementses should have let their kids have more freedom. Then they might not have to get cuddly with the staff."

"That's for sure. Why did you bring Ivy? We probably could have all squished in the truck and made it home."

"Maria didn't kill Silvia," I said.

José let out a slow breath through his nose. "Of course she didn't."

Jett leaned against the truck. "I'm still pretty certain she blew up the truck."

"I bet it was Kyle."

"That's the way I'm leaning," I said.

Jett nodded. "But what about whatever Jennifer did?"

I hugged myself for warmth, and Jett came over and put his arm around me.

"What if you call everyone together and talk to them, and I search some of their rooms?" I suggested.

"I can do that. Do we want them to know we know Maria didn't kill Silvia?"

I rubbed my lips together. "If they think they got away with it, that might be better. They won't be on their guard."

"Let's do it," José said. "I miss the diner."

Chapter 13

José told Eric to round everyone up and have them meet in the dining room. I found Boyd, and once we were sure they were all in the same area, we went to Jennifer's room.

"What are we looking for?" Boyd asked as I handed him some gloves Jett had brought.

"Anything weird." I opened the closet, and my eyes went wide. The closet was almost as big as my bedroom. I walked in and pushed some things around. It was all neatly organized, and there wasn't anywhere to hide anything.

"Ivy?" Boyd said. I went out and saw Boyd's feet sticking out from under the bed.

"Did you find something?"

"Maybe, but I'm stuck."

With a smile, I grabbed Boyd's feet and slid him out from under the bed. It wasn't easy, but the slick floors helped.

"Something is under the bed. I think you can pull up a piece of the floor, and something will be hidden there."

I laughed. "I think you've seen too many movies."

"I'm serious. I can tell the floor's been tampered with."

"Alright. Let's move the bed." I grabbed one of the wooden bedposts and pulled. It barely moved. "It's heavy." I pulled again, and Boyd went to the other side and pushed. It moved a few more inches.

Boyd shook his head. "I don't think we're going to get it."

I pushed the bed back into place and pulled off the mattress. "Now I'm going to have to make the bed." I stepped into the bed frame and looked at the wooden planks. Boyd was right. A square appeared to have been cut out and put back in.

Boyd grinned. "I told you. I bet she has something hidden in there."

I got down on my hands and knees and worked on prying the piece out with my fingernails. "I wish I had a screwdriver."

"I should have gotten you a Swiss army knife for Christmas instead of a cat statue."

"I love that cat statue," I said, cringing when the side of my fingernail tore too low.

"As much as you love your cat apron?"

I smiled. "It's much cuter than the apron."

"Someday, you gotta burn that apron or tell Jett he has bad taste."

"I already told him it was hideous." The board began coming up, then it slipped.

"Did he cry?"

"No." It came up again, and I stuck my hand under it and pulled. A few boards came up, leaving a perfect square. I looked down and frowned. After pulling out my phone, I stuck my head in and shined the flashlight down.

"What's in there?" Boyd asked.

"It's a tunnel. It goes down a few feet, then goes so far I can't see the end. It must go between this floor and the ceiling on the lower floor."

"That doesn't sound safe."

"I'm going," I said. I lowered myself in and got on my hands and knees. It was going to be dark. I wished I had a headlamp.

"Crawl quietly," Boyd said, looking down at me. "You're going to be over people's heads, and they might hear you."

"I doubt this goes over the dining room. That's clear on the other side of the house."

"I'll come with you."

"Don't. You stay here and keep watch. I don't know how long Jett can keep everyone in one place."

"It might be dangerous. What if the floor's weak?"

"Someone's been coming here. It isn't all dusty or any-thing."

I put my phone in my mouth. It wouldn't be great for light that way, but better than nothing. I crawled quickly and soon came to a turn. My knees and hands were getting sore. I followed the tunnel until it ended. There was a slight drop-off and then a tiny room.

Dropping down, I found a light switch and flipped it. The room was only about six feet by six feet. It had a small round table with dolls sitting on chairs in front of little tea cups. Framed pictures of teddy bears decorated two of the walls. This must have been an out-of-the-way play area for Jennifer and Amanda when they were young.

Across from me was another tunnel in the wall. I would almost bet it went to Amanda's room. I smiled. What a fun idea. I would have loved this when I was young. I picked up the teakettle and heard something move inside. Opening the lid, I saw a small bottle. I pulled it out and looked at the label.

"Diphenhydramine," I read out loud. "Liquid sleep aid." I snapped a picture with my phone. Now would be a good time to have cell service so I could send it to someone. I put it back and looked around the room. Nothing else stood out as being weird.

Boosting myself back into the tunnel, I crawled back the way I'd come. Jett probably struggled to keep everyone together, and I still had other rooms to check. The sleeping aid had to mean something. Lots of people used sleep aids, but this one was hidden. When I got closer, I saw something ahead. I paused and shined my light.

"Boyd?" The bottom part of Boyd was in the tunnel, and the top must still be in Jennifer's room. He was kneeling, and his arms were still up above. "What are you doing?" I moved closer.

"I'm stuck," Boyd said. "Super stuck. I'm like a pig. A pig that's really stuck in a hole, or something. I forget the saying."

I rolled my eyes. "You have to go up."

"Can't. Not up or down. We're gonna have to break the floor."

"We can't break the floor. Everyone will know we were here."

"Did you find anything?"

"Maybe. We don't have time. You have to try harder."

"It's not happening."

I sighed. "Alright. There's a path going out another way. I'll be back." I turned, crawled as fast as I could, and dropped into the playroom. Once there, I boosted myself into the tunnel on the other side. It had to go somewhere. I crawled until I came to a dead end.

"This better be it," I muttered. I shined my light up and saw a similar square to the one in Jennifer's room. I pushed up, and the floor came up. Relief flooded me when I didn't come up under a bed. After climbing into a bedroom, I put the piece of flooring back. I didn't take the time to study the room. I hurried out the door and back to Boyd.

I entered, and he grinned. He was up to his armpits in the floor.

"That was fast," he said.

Looking down at the floor, I frowned. There was no way I was getting him out of this.

"The way I see it, it's your fault," Boyd said.

I tilted my head. "How is this my fault?"

He chuckled. "If you didn't make so many cookies, I would be thinner."

"Ha ha. I'm going to have to get Jett."

"How do you keep everyone else away?"

I shrugged. "I could get José, but Jett's more likely to be able to pull you out or something."

There was no reason to wait around and argue, so I hurried out of the room and off to the dining room.

I peeked in, and everyone was eating cookies. Jett must have been telling them something boring because no one was listening. When he saw me, he excused himself and came to the door.

"We found a secret passage in Jennifer's and Amanda's rooms," I whispered. "Boyd got stuck in it."

Jett squeezed his eyes shut and rubbed his temples. "Alright, just a minute." He turned back to the people. "I'll be back in a few minutes. I don't want anyone to leave until I get back."

"Why?" Kyle asked. "You already have the murderer."

"It's not that simple. No one is to leave this room, do you understand?"

They all nodded, and Jett and I started for Jennifer's room.

"I'm sorry. I bet they're all getting antsy," I said.

"Actually, it's amazing what your cookies can do. I think they're all happy to sit there eating them. I guess Silvia was a real stickler about no cookies. She was happy to have dessert so long as it looked elegant, and cookies are for poor people in her opinion."

"Well, I guess that's a good thing."

"Did you find anything?"

"I followed the passage and found a little playroom. It links Jennifer's and Amanda's rooms together. In the playroom was a little tea set, and I found a bottle of a sleep aid in the teakettle."

"Interesting," he said, following me up the stairs.

"I know people use sleep aids a lot, but why would it be hidden in there? It seems suspicious to me."

We entered Jennifer's room, and Jett put his hands on his hips. "What are you doing, Boyd?"

"Just hanging out," he said, grinning up at them.

Jett walked over and stepped over the bed frame. "Boyd, you aren't young. You know this. You have to stop climbing up things and in things. What if we have to cut the floor? How do we explain that?"

"You don't have to," Lionel said from behind me.

Jett turned. "I told everyone to stay put."

"Yes, but I could tell something was wrong. You are welcome to search anywhere in the house. Get him out however you feel is best. Cut him out, butter him, whatever."

I giggled when I thought of coating Boyd in butter, and Jett shot me a look. "I'm going to leave this to you," I said. There were so many rooms in this place that it would be almost impossible to search them all. Jett had been through them, but I wasn't sure how thoroughly he was able to be with the time we'd had.

Amanda's room was the next logical choice. I would search Eric's, but I didn't know where it was. I went to Amanda's and glanced around. This looked like the room of a teenager, not a woman in her forties. There were pictures of pop stars on the walls. Most of them I didn't know. They were professionally framed. The bed wasn't made, but that could be because Kyle had fired the maids. I doubted Callie was still cleaning if she was no longer employed here.

Aside from the bed, the room was spotless.

An enormous bookcase was lined with books in height order. One book was pulled out farther than the others. I thought of all the movies with books that actually opened secret passages. I grabbed the book and pulled it from the shelf. Nothing happened. The book felt wrong, though, so I turned it around. It was fake.

My heart pounded as I wondered what could be inside. I pulled it open and gasped. Inside was a bloody knife.

Chapter 14

Everyone sat around the table, waiting for Jett to speak. Jett and Lionel had managed to get Boyd out of the floor without anyone being the wiser, and he sat next to José and Anton.

Jett set the false book on the table, his gloves going a few inches past his hands. "Does anyone recognize this book?" he asked.

Everyone stared at the book. Amanda didn't look more curious or guilty than anyone else.

"No? How about this?" he asked, holding up the sleeping aid. I'd gone back and gotten it for him. There was no way he would have fit.

Jennifer swallowed hard and looked at Eric. He shook his head slightly, and she looked down.

"Come on," Jett said. "Someone knows something."

My eyes went from Jennifer to Eric, and I tried to remember the conversation I'd overheard.

Jett tapped his foot against the floor. "There is a lot of garbage going on at this house. Let's air it all out. Anyone want to start? Come on. Don't make me start guessing."

"Kyle's the biggest problem around here," Callie declared.

"Shut up," Kyle said, glaring at her. "You're the help. You don't get to talk."

Lionel slammed his hand against the table. "You will not talk to people that way!"

Kyle slumped down in his chair and crossed his arms.

"You know better than to enter into relationships with the staff," Lionel said. "I can't count the times I've told you that."

"I'm forty years old! I can date anyone I want."

"And all at the same time." Callie glared at Kyle.

He shrugged. "Jennifer and Eric have been in a relationship for years, and no one is bringing that up."

Jennifer looked up at her dad, and he frowned.

"Jennifer was also drugging her aunt so she could spend time with Eric," Jett said. I knew he didn't know for sure, but he was making a confident guess.

Jennifer covered her mouth, and her eyes went wide.

"And Eric knew about it," Jett added.

Eric chewed the side of his cheek but didn't say anything.

"I didn't kill Silvia," Jennifer stated.

Jett nodded. "Perhaps not, but it's illegal to give a person a sleep aid without their knowledge."

Jennifer sniffled. "Aunt Silvia was a beast! Everyone knows it. She didn't want any of us to date anyone. She never let us do anything unless it made her look good!"

"Jennifer," Lionel said with a warning tone.

"No! You let your sister rule us all. You're to blame almost as much as she is. What kind of father keeps their grown children from living their lives?"

Lionel sighed and put a hand to his head.

"Did I drug Silvia?" Jennifer asked. "Yes, all the time. Am I sorry? No. I didn't kill her, though."

The room went silent. Eric was looking down at his hands, and Kyle smirked.

"You gave her the sleep aid the night she died," Jett said.

"Yes. Then Maria killed her."

"Maria didn't kill her," Jett said. "At least I don't think so."

Callie frowned. "Everyone knows it was Maria."

"She blew up my truck, but she didn't kill anyone."

"Why blow up the truck?" Lionel asked.

"To destroy any evidence that Kyle might have done it."

Kyle glared. "I didn't do it."

"Maybe not, but Maria thinks you did, and she was trying to protect you even after you were a jerk to her."

"That's all on her. I didn't do anything. Why would I kill my mom? I would get all her money anyway, and now I'm going to have to share it with all these people. It wouldn't benefit me anything."

"Let's go back to the book," Jett said, holding up the fake book in his gloved hand. "Anyone recognize this?"

Everyone shook their heads. He opened it and pulled out the bloody knife. Jennifer and Amanda gasped, and Lionel frowned.

"This was in Amanda's room."

Amanda's eyes went wide, then she glared at Eric.

Eric's mouth turned down. "Why are you looking at me like that?"

She didn't answer.

"Do you have anything to say?" Jett asked her.

"No."

"Nothing?"

She shrugged. "Nothing."

"Did you kill Silvia?"

She pushed her brown hair over her shoulder. "I'm not talking to you without a lawyer."

Jett nodded. "Fine. None of this is going the way it should since I can't get more officers or forensics in here. I was able to use a satellite phone to call and let the police in Wichita know what was happening. This place will be swarming with people as soon as the roads are clear."

Kyle looked at his uncle. "We can't have that, Lionel. We'll have all sorts of bad press."

Lionel shrugged. "I don't see any way to avoid it."

Eric had a small smile on his face.

"How many people know about the other will?" Kyle asked. "That's going to make us look bad when people find out my mom changed it."

"Money is the root of all evil," Clint said. "Isn't that what the Bible says? And we've all seen it. I married Silvia for her money, and I haven't been happy a day since. Yes, I said it. I only married her for the money. If I could go back in time, I would tell myself to run and never look back."

"What does money have to do with anything?" Kyle asked. "That has nothing to do with any of this."

"Sure it does," Clint said. "If Silvia hadn't been greedy and changed the will, maybe Amanda wouldn't have felt the need to stab her. I don't blame you one bit," he said, taking a drink from his bottle and looking at Amanda.

Amanda's eyes narrowed, but she didn't speak.

I watched everyone at the table closely. Amanda had honestly looked surprised when Jett said the knife was in her room. She hadn't denied anything, though.

"Is anyone who lives here happy?" Clint asked. "Not a single person. None of us even like each other." He pulled a crumpled-up piece of paper from his pocket and waved it in the air. "You wanna know why you all are the way you are? Read your letters from Grandpa Zeb."

"What do they say?" Jett asked.

Clint handed the letter to him. "This is Silvia's. She crumpled it up and threw it away, but I pulled it out of the trash. Everyone got a letter when he died."

"I threw mine away as soon as I read it," Kyle said. "Grandpa was a jerk."

"So did I," Jennifer admitted.

I looked at Jett. "What does it say?"

He glanced down. "Silvia, I won't say dear because we know that's a lie, and detested Silvia sounds a bit cruel. I know why you are the way you are. You're just like me. That's why we don't get along. I know you messed with my will, but I'm too old and tired to do anything about it. Return the will to its original state, or I'm sure you will meet with a less-than-satisfactory end. I wouldn't put it past anyone in this house to do something drastic. From your father, Zebadiah James Clements."

"Mine was about as loving as that," Kyle offered.

"No one misses him or Silvia," Clint said.

"With Silvia gone, I can be with Eric," Jennifer explained. "I don't care what the rest of you say." Eric nodded.

"How are you going to be with him when you're in prison for drugging your aunt?" Lionel asked.

Jennifer frowned.

Eric took Jennifer's hand. "I'll wait for you, no matter what."

"We've all let things get out of control," Lionel declared. "I think the best thing this family can do after the will is all figured out is get away from one another."

"I'm not against that," Kyle said. "I'm sick of all of you."

"The feeling is mutual," Clint said.

"Thanks, Dad. I thought I might have you on my side."

"You chose your side when you chose to take the Clements name instead of mine."

"Do I have to be here?" Anton asked.

"I want plenty of witnesses to all of this," Jett said.

"How much longer do we have to stay here?" Jennifer asked.

Jett scratched his chin. "I suppose you can all go. No one is to leave this property until the roads are plowed and there is a full investigation."

"Do you want us to keep cooking?" I asked Lionel.

"If you would, I'd appreciate it. I know it's been longer than we contracted you, but I will pay."

I nodded.

"Any chance you make brownies?" Kyle asked.

Boyd grinned. "That's like asking Chef Boyardee if he makes canned pasta. Ivy's brownies are the best."

I wasn't sure how I felt about my baking being compared to canned pasta. "Thanks, Boyd. I'll go make some." I went to the kitchen, pulled out the ingredients, and set them on the island. It felt weird to be baking for a bunch of possible criminals.

"I bet this is the craziest catering experience you've ever had," Eric said, entering the kitchen. He sat on a stool and watched me prepare.

I grabbed the flour and a measuring cup. "This is my first catering experience, actually."

He laughed softly. "I hope it won't be your last. You're all good at what you do."

"Thank you." I dumped the flour into the bowl and picked up the salt. My opinion of Eric had changed. He had to have known Jennifer was drugging Silvia. I'd watched their silent communication at the table. If he was going to let her go down alone, he lost all my respect. He should at least admit he was aware of it.

"It's nice you and Jennifer don't have to hide things anymore," I said. I had no evidence to say Eric had done anything more than know about Jennifer drugging Silvia, but I had a strong feeling he was more guilty than that. I just didn't know exactly how.

Jett peeked into the kitchen, and when he saw Eric, he backed out. I was eighty percent sure he was listening at the door.

"Jennifer and I have been together for years, but mostly from necessity."

I narrowed my eyes. "What does that mean?"

"Working here is a dream job. The Clementses like to be better than everyone else and that includes paying their employees. I've made enough money here to retire comfortably in a few years. The Clementses are really strict, though. I don't get much time off, so I have no social life. That's really the only reason I stay with Jennifer. It was either her or Amanda."

"You just told her you would wait for her if she went to jail."

He shrugged. "I probably will."

I couldn't believe I'd ever said Eric was decent. "Aren't you in love with her?"

"Not at all."

"I thought you were one of the better people here. I guess I was wrong."

He stood and came up close to me. "I am better. Don't you see what a service I did for Jennifer? She would have spent years feeling lonely."

Eric was delusional.

"Jennifer can marry anyone she wants now that Silvia's gone. She might not be attractive, but she'll have millions."

"You aren't helping me feel better about you," I said, mixing the dry ingredients. "And there's nothing wrong with the way she looks."

"I'll probably marry her. Don't think poorly of me."

I raised my eyebrow and kept stirring. "Marry her for her money?"

"No. I told you I have plenty. Still, I can't help thinking there might be someone better for me out there." He rubbed my arm, and I stepped away. He was not good at picking up the vibes in the room.

"Come on," he said. "I know we had a connection."

"We didn't."

"I know you think you have the sheriff, but anyone can see that's not going anywhere. He's paying attention to you for the same reason I pay attention to Jennifer. Muddy Creek isn't full of young ladies. He probably staked his claim on you the second you moved in because someone was finally attractive in that pathetic town."

He touched my arm again, and I moved it away. "Don't touch me."

"This was all too sudden, wasn't it? I like you, Ivy. I'm better than the sheriff, but I don't have time to prove it to you. That's why I'm moving fast."

"You literally just said you were probably going to marry Jennifer."

"Not if I find someone better." He ran his finger over my cheek, and I turned and smacked him in the face with my mixing bowl. Surprised, he stumbled back, and flour and cocoa powder coated everything in a cloud.

Eric put a hand to his face, but before he could say anything, Jett barged into the room. He grabbed Eric by the collar and whisked him to the door. He kicked it open and pushed Eric out.

"Don't come near her again!" he yelled. I couldn't see out the doorway but heard footsteps quickly retreating.

I stood in the floury mess and sighed.

"What happened?" Jett asked, pointing at the floor. "I was listening, but I wasn't exactly sure what was going on."

"I told him not to touch me. He did, so I hit him in the face with my mixing bowl."

Jett nodded and grabbed a broom from the closet. "And we thought he was the normal one. We need to get out of here. The only person who seems halfway decent is Lionel." He swept up my mess.

"I think Eric did it."

"What?"

"Killed Silvia. I know there's absolutely no evidence, but I bet he did."

"But the knife was in Amanda's room, and she won't deny doing it."

"Eric must have something over her. She knows, and she isn't saying it."

He sighed. "I need to get everyone out of here. It's all too dangerous."

Chapter 15

The sun shone in from the window, and I forced myself to climb out of bed. A loud scraping noise came from outside. I pulled back the curtains and smiled. It wasn't snowing, not even flurries. Off in the distance, I could see a truck moving back and forth. Hal must be plowing the road. I hurried and got ready for the day, then went to Jett's room and knocked on the door.

"Come in," he said.

I opened it and found him standing beside his window, staring out. He glanced back at me, then back outside.

"Is that Hal out there?"

"Yes."

I went to stand by him and looked out. "Does that mean we can leave?"

He nodded. "I'll have Hal take Anton and Boyd back with him. I need to take Amanda to the jail. That only leaves one spot in the truck, and I still need to get you and José back. I don't want to leave either of you here alone."

"What about Eric and Jennifer?"

He sighed. "It's all a mess."

"I can take my car if the road is clear."

"Your car's buried. It will take some work to get it out. I think Hal covered it even more than it was. Maybe I should have José take you and Boyd back, then come back. This is all such a disaster. I've done too many things wrong."

I frowned. "You're doing fine."

"I lost a body, found the body, and had the body get burned up. Now, whatever's left is just sitting outside in a burned-up pile covered in a tarp and snow. Amanda might be guilty, Jennifer's guilty of something, and I just feel tired."

"Maybe José should take Boyd and Anton back and bring Deputy Ledford. He might be some help."

"I suppose. But then nobody is watching the rest of the town."

"I'm surprised Muddy Creek comes clear out here."

"I'm not sure this is Muddy Creek. It's too far to actually count, but everyone still calls it Muddy Creek. There are so many little towns around, I'm not sure what town this counts as."

"Then do you have jurisdiction here?"

"Yes. I'm the sheriff of the county, not just Muddy Creek. It just feels like it's only Muddy Creek because there isn't a lot out here, so most of my work is there."

A Mercedes turned into the driveway and began moving slowly up to the house. I'd seen it around town, but I wasn't sure who it belonged to.

"That's just great," Jett muttered.

"Who is it?"

"Mayor Jepson."

"I've never met him."

"He comes to the diner some Saturdays. He's a large man who always sits in the corner and doesn't talk to anyone."

"Oh, okay. I've wondered about him. He doesn't seem very social."

"He's not. That's why everyone ignores him when he comes in. He doesn't like to be approached. He thinks he's a celebrity or something. He's told people more than once that he doesn't want to be approached in public because he's busy thinking about important things."

"How did he get elected?"

"Same way I did. No one else ran against him. I better go talk to him." He turned and walked from the room. I followed a short distance behind. We walked through the house and into the entryway.

Mayor Jepson was taking off his boots and muttering something. Eric showed him where to put them. He tossed the boots into the wooden box and glared at Jett.

"Hello, Mayor," Jett said.

"I need a word." He looked at Eric. "Is there anywhere I can speak privately with the sheriff?"

"Of course," Eric said. With his perfect posture and neat suit, he seemed like the proper butler again. He led them to a room off to the side and pointed in. Jett and Mayor Jepson disappeared inside and closed the door.

I couldn't listen at the door while Eric was there, so I hoped he would leave.

"Good to see you this morning, Miss Clark." He nodded his head and walked away, ignoring the fact that he had a line on his face from where I'd hit him with my mixing bowl.

I shrugged. If that was how he was going to play it, I was fine with that. I walked up to the door and put my ear close. I'd done more eavesdropping on this trip than I wanted to admit. If I were the Clementses, I would make my house a little more soundproof.

The mayor sounded like he was lecturing Jett, but I missed the first part.

"It's under control," Jett said.

"Oh? That's not how it sounded when I talked to Deputy Ledford. This will turn into a high-profile case, and I don't want our town looking bad."

"No offense, Mayor, but I don't answer to you."

"Maybe not, but you need to think of what type of message our town sends to the rest of the world."

"This is all going to be fine. I'm on top of it. Ledford hasn't been here. He only knows a little of what's happening."

"Well, the murderer is in jail, so at least we have that. Ledford said that you let the body get destroyed."

"I'm doing the best I can with what I have, and Maria isn't the murderer. She blew up my truck, but as far as I can tell, that's her only crime."

"Then where is the murderer?"

"Once again, I don't answer to you."

"There is also the concern about your conduct with the diner woman."

I frowned. That was an unflattering title.

"There's nothing inappropriate about my relationship with Ivy. Even if there was, it's still not your business."

"Leford says you've been spending time with her when you're on duty. What type of message does that send to your voters?"

"When am I not on duty?" Jett asked, his voice rising. "I get calls day and night. I'm on call all the time."

"Then you should avoid having a social life until you leave this job. People are talking."

"People or Ledford?"

"It doesn't matter who it comes from. Part of holding a public office is upholding your image. You know the media is going to blow Silvia Clements's murder up all over the country. Do you really want to be the sheriff who didn't do all he could to solve the mystery because he was busy cuddling with the diner owner?"

"You don't know what you're talking about," Jett growled. "You only know what Ledford told you, and he's not the best source of information."

"You know Ledford's going to run against you in the next election?"

"I'm not threatened by Ledford. His approval rating in the town is almost as low as yours."

I cringed. Jett wasn't endearing himself to the man.

"I'm done with this conversation," Jett said.

I tiptoed quickly across the floor to get out of sight. I went around the corner and made my way to the kitchen. José was frying eggs, Boyd gazed out the window, and Anton sat at the table with his head down.

"Are we getting out of here?" José asked.

"I think so. Hal plowed the road. Jett is trying to come up with a strategy that would allow everyone to leave without abandoning anyone or leaving any suspects behind."

"Where is he now?" José asked.

"The mayor came. The two of them are arguing."

Boyd chuckled. "Mayor Jepson argues with everyone."

I sat next to Anton. "I've never met him, but I've seen him at the diner."

Anton looked up. "Boyd should run for mayor."

Boyd laughed. "I don't know anything about that kind of stuff."

"You'd still be better than Jepson. I bet anyone could beat him. People dislike him almost as much as Ledford."

Jett came in frowning. "We need to leave. I've convinced the mayor to take José, Boyd, and Anton back in his car. I'll stay here with Ivy and dig out her car. If one of you could get Ledford to come, we can take Amanda and Jennifer in."

"What about Eric?" I asked.

"I can't arrest him because you think he's guilty. It doesn't work that way."

Anton rested his elbow on the table. "I thought it was Kyle, but if Ivy says it's Eric, I'm with her."

I smiled. "You get to keep your job whether you agree with me or not."

He grinned. "I know. I'll just be glad to put this all behind me. You're usually right. I'm not cut out for this type of thing."

Lionel came into the kitchen in a red polo shirt and slacks. He looked tired. "I saw the plow. I've locked the garage and have all the keys so no one can leave."

"Thank you," Jett said. Lionel nodded and left.

"He's pretty mellow for a guy whose daughters are both about to go to jail," Boyd said.

I began gathering all my supplies. "I don't think the family dynamics around here are healthy."

"I'm almost finished with breakfast," José said. "Is the mayor in a hurry?"

Boyd raised his brow. "I doubt he is if he can get a free breakfast."

Chapter 16

Snow surrounded me, and I was sweating. Lionel had given us shovels, and Jett and I were digging out my car. José, Boyd, and Anton had left with the mayor, and we were waiting for Ledford to come so Jett could officially arrest Jennifer and Amanda.

I took off my puffy coat and tossed it to the ground. It was hard to dig around the car and not scratch the paint. My mind went back to the mayor's conversation with Jett. I tried to block it from my mind, but I couldn't help wondering if I was ruining Jett's image.

I rolled my eyes. I couldn't see how the town could be judging us. Jett had never kissed me until we were here. The only person who could be spreading rumors was Ledford. I thought about all the teasing we'd been getting from our friends. I'd tried to play it off, but my feelings must have been more obvious than I thought.

"There's Ledford," Jett said, pointing. I looked down the road and saw a black Dodge Charger coming toward us.

Ledford pulled up next to us, then rolled down his window and looked at us through his glasses. "Who am I arresting?"

Jett stuck his shovel in the snow. "Meet me up at the house."

Ledford nodded and drove up the long driveway. Jett jogged to catch up, and I kept digging. I wasn't confident about getting the car out. Once we uncovered it, it would still have a bunch of snow underneath.

Grumbling to myself, I kept shoveling. Anton was the one who had gotten the car into this mess, and now he was probably home taking a nap. I shouldn't judge Anton. This experience had shaken him, and I couldn't blame him for getting out as fast as he could. If my life kept going the way it had since I came to Muddy Creek, I would have to start giving my employees hazard pay.

Two vans came from the opposite direction of town and turned into the driveway. I watched them pull up to the house, and several people got out. Jett stood out front doing something. I imagined putting Amanda and Jennifer into Ledford's car. I couldn't see well enough, and I was missing everything.

Ten minutes passed, and Jett came jogging back to me. "The forensic people are here. I'm going to need to talk to them for a while. Are you alright out here on your own? You can come in and wait, and I can do the rest later."

"No, I'll keep going. The sooner I dig us out, the sooner we can leave."

He nodded and headed back to the house.

After five more minutes, I was ready to give up. The car was mostly uncovered, but still needed to have the windows cleared better, and I needed to shovel around it so we could get to the plowed area. My arms were throbbing.

"Need some help?" I spun around to see Eric standing there with a shovel.

"No, I'm fine."

He began shoveling a path toward the plowed area of the road.

"Go back to the house," I said. Eric was the last person I wanted to be alone with, especially when he was holding a shovel.

"That wouldn't be very chivalrous of me."

"It actually would because it's what I want."

He ignored me and kept shoveling.

"Shouldn't you be seeing Jennifer off?" I asked.

"I've been thinking. Jennifer isn't really the one for me. It would be a lie to both of us."

"And you're going to let her go to jail and not tell anyone that you knew exactly what she was doing?"

Eric looked over his shoulder and frowned at me. "What do you mean?"

"You knew she was drugging her aunt. She was doing it to spend time with you."

"I might have suspected."

"No, you knew."

He grinned. "What evidence do you have? None. It's all your opinion."

"What do you have over Amanda? She didn't know the knife was in her room, but she looked at you and kept her mouth shut."

He laughed. "Wait, are you saying I killed Silvia?"

I didn't say anything. I just kept shoveling.

"Wow," he said. "You do think it was me. I'm surprised you haven't had your little sheriff throw me in jail."

"Little? He's bigger and stronger than you. He tossed you out of the kitchen yesterday like you were a bag of trash."

He glared at me but kept shoveling. "When should I expect to get arrested?"

I tossed my shovel, then pried open the passenger side door and grabbed my window scraper. "You shouldn't. Jett won't arrest you because he doesn't think you did it, and there isn't any evidence." I began scraping the ice from the windshield. The sound gave me the chills, but I kept going.

"I guess I'm safe then. Why would you think it was me and not Kyle? He's the type. Playboy rich kid whose mommy isn't giving him everything he feels entitled to. He has a temper too. I wouldn't be shocked if he was behind it all."

"Yes, you would since you know you did it." I knew my speculations weren't sound, and I was flat-out accusing someone of murder when there was no evidence, but I was tired and ready to be done with this case.

"Why are you so sure it's me?"

"I've been watching you when things happen. Your facial expressions aren't just those of the concerned butler boyfriend." I wasn't getting all the ice off, but I kept trying. My old home in Arizona sounded nice right about now.

Eric shoveled some snow onto my coat. "Dang." He picked up my coat and shook it. My car key fell out. He picked it up and returned it to the pocket and put it on the hood of the car.

"I've been nothing but nice to you," he said. "I don't know why you suddenly see me as a criminal."

"You were nice until you started talking crazy yesterday."

"You're just upset because I'm not crazy about Jennifer. Relationships change. I haven't been able to think about her since you came."

"I haven't been here that long. You don't know me."

"Well, I like what I do know and definitely what I see."

"You're a creep." I turned and began walking to the house. I wasn't staying with him any longer.

He grabbed my arm and stopped me. I tried to pull free, but he had a good grip.

"Let go."

"Get in the car."

"No. Jett!" I yelled. There was little chance he would hear me, but I thought I might scare Eric. Ledford's car was coming down the driveway. I waved my free arm at him. He waved and drove past. "Stop!" I yelled. "Are you kidding me!"

Eric laughed. "Now, get in the car." I pulled back and fell into the snow. Eric opened the back door to the car while I scrambled to my feet. I turned to run, but Eric held a gun. "Get in the car."

I doubted he would shoot me, but not enough to test it. I climbed into the back seat. He threw my coat in at me and slammed the door. He got into the driver's seat and started the car. He didn't need the key since it had a wireless key fob, and the key was in the car.

"If you do this, everyone will know you're the killer."

"No, they'll know we ran off together. It happens all the time." He pulled onto the slick road and drove slowly in the opposite direction of Muddy Creek.

"Jett's not stupid. He knows how I feel about you." I pulled my key from my pocket and rolled down the window. I threw it as hard as I could into the snow.

"That was stupid," Eric said. "Tossing the key doesn't stop the car."

I frowned. I really thought it would. "Well, next time you stop, you won't be able to start it again."

"Then I won't stop until I get where I want to."

"Good luck. There's only about forty miles of gas."

He sighed. "It's dangerous not to keep your tank full. What if you got stranded in the snow?"

We hadn't gotten far, but the farther we got, the worse things looked for me. I had to get out now. I could hit Eric with the window scraper, but I didn't see that being very effective. There was a lot of snow. I could jump. We were going slow enough that it probably wouldn't hurt. I looked out the back window and saw a forensic van following.

Opening the door, I jumped. I rolled away from the road. I wasn't hurt at all. Eric stopped the car, but he must have seen the van behind us because he took off, sliding around the road. He stabilized it and moved forward.

Getting to my feet, I brushed the snow from my jeans. The van stopped, and Jett jumped out.

He ran over and wrapped me in a hug. "Are you alright?"

"Fine. Eric stole my car."

"I don't care about your car." He kissed the top of my head. "I'm going to call Wichita and have them watch for him. He's headed in that direction. I'll never catch up in that van."

"Are the phones working?"

"Yep."

"There isn't a lot of gas in the car. He won't get far."

Jett nodded and got on his phone. I took a deep breath. I still couldn't believe Ledford drove right past. He had to have known I was in trouble. When Jett finished, we went back up to the house.

"I need to get you home," he said. He came to the kitchen to help me get my things. The forensic people were all over checking things. When we got to the entryway, I pulled on my shoes, and I seriously hoped this was the last time I would ever step foot in here.

"This is it," Jett said. "Everything goes back to normal after we leave." He put his arms around me and leaned down, pressing his warm lips to mine. I rested my hands on his shoulders, but my mind wasn't completely in the kiss. Was he saying once we left the house, that was the end of whatever we'd had here?

My heart felt heavy. That had to be what he meant. I'd been right. What happened at the Clementses' stayed at the Clementses'.

Chapter 17

By the time I reached my bed, I was completely drained. I'd never been so happy to have Creepers sleep on my face. I'd expected to fall asleep immediately, but my mind had been racing even before Jett dropped me off. All I could take from our last conversation was that whatever we'd had was over now. Jett hadn't come out and said it, but that was what I understood.

Creepers positioned himself so I couldn't roll over. I picked him up and moved him next to me, then rolled to my side. He batted at the back of my head, then crawled over me and pushed his head to mine.

"I know. I've been gone too long. I don't think catering was the best idea. Tomorrow, we go back to normal, alright?" He meowed. "What is normal?" I ran my hand over his gray fur. My eyes felt heavy, and I closed them. It didn't take long to fall asleep to Creeper's purring.

The following morning, I was ready for the day. I went downstairs to the smell of bacon and two tables of customers. I'd meant to text José and tell him we'd be open today, but I'd forgotten. It seemed he'd figured that was what I wanted.

"Morning," I said, walking into the kitchen.

"Good morning," José said. He was flipping eggs, and Carrie was frying bacon.

"Where's Anton?" I asked.

José chuckled. "He said he needs a week off. I figured the poor kid deserves it."

"Kid?"

"You're all kids to me."

"I doubt we'll have too many people. The roads might be plowed, but we still slid all over last night."

"Yeah, I doubt we'll see Boyd. His electric bike might be fancy, but we've had too much snow."

I frowned. "I feel bad when Boyd can't come. I think he's too lonely when he can't come to town."

"Yeah. He should sell his house and move to town. He's getting too old for some of the things he does."

Carrie piled bacon on a plate. "There are a lot of rumors going around town right now."

"Oh?" I asked.

"People are saying half the Clementses are in jail. I figure it's just a rumor."

"I wouldn't say half," José said. "Only two."

"Really? What happened?"

José began telling Carrie about the past few days. I tuned them out and made some cookies. Every time the front doors opened, I peeked out the window into the dining area to see if it was Jett. I had to find out if Eric had been caught.

There wasn't much to do once the customers were all served. José was still telling Carrie about the Clementses, and I began to feel restless. I didn't want to be in here baking. I wanted to know what was going on.

Carrie laughed at something José said, and I paused. I'd never paid attention to the way my employees interacted. Carrie looked delighted by José's retelling of the week, and José was more animated than normal. Was there something there I hadn't noticed before? I was going to pay more attention.

Boyd came in covered in snow.

"What are you doing?" I asked. "You didn't ride your bike, did you?"

"Naw, I got a ride. What happened to your car? I just saw the tow truck bring it over."

"Oh good," I said, washing my hands. "Did it look alright?"

"Fine. What happened to it?"

"Eric stole it."

"What?"

I gave them a quick version of what had happened after they left.

"I knew it!" Boyd exclaimed. "The butler is always guilty."

"We still don't know if he killed Silvia," I said, trying to be fair.

"Course he did. Why else would he try to leave? Everyone knew they needed to stay at the mansion until all the police work was finished."

"I can't believe we didn't make Ledford stop for you," José said. "I wasn't paying a lot of attention when we drove off."

"I just thought you were lecturing him," said Boyd.

"While he held on to my arm?"

"I didn't notice that. Sorry."

"It's fine. It worked out, except I don't know if anyone caught Eric."

The door opened, and Barbra entered with her friend Opal. She waved at all of us behind the window. "Hello in there! We've missed you." A server led them to a table.

"I'll be out there," Boyd said, leaving the kitchen and going to sit with Barbra.

"Do you think those two will ever get together?" Carrie asked.

"I wish," José said. "They've been flirting for years. They should get married so they wouldn't have to be so lonely."

"Do you ever get lonely, living on your own?" I asked José.

"Not too bad. I spend most of my time here."

"Why haven't you ever gotten married?" I knew I was prying, but he deserved it after all the times he'd teased me. I noticed Carrie cleaning the counter and trying to look like she wasn't listening.

He chuckled. "I've just always been busy. Now I'm too old."

"You're way younger than Boyd."

He shrugged. "I guess so. Jett's and your relationship has sure changed these past few days."

Great. It was back on me. "Mistletoe doesn't mean anything," I said, trying to remember if he'd seen anything besides that first kiss.

"That was like no mistletoe kiss I've ever seen. Poor Anton almost had to leave the room."

Carrie giggled. "I want to hear about this."

"I don't," I said. "I'm going to find Jett and see if they caught Eric." Grabbing my coat, I left the diner. The sheriff's office wouldn't be a great place to talk. Ledford might be there, and Jennifer, Amanda, and Maria were probably locked up inside.

I walked into the building and tried not to frown when I saw Ledford at the desk typing something on the computer. He glanced up at me but didn't say anything.

"Is Jett here?"

"*Sheriff* Malone is back with the prisoners."

I nodded and walked into the back. Jett faced the two cells with his hands on his hips. Jennifer sat on a bed with puffy red eyes, and Amanda stood by with her arms crossed, glaring at Jett. Maria was in the other cell, lying on the bed and staring at the ceiling.

He turned when I entered. "Hey, Ivy."

"Can I talk to them for a minute?" I asked.

He threw his hands in the air. "Sure, but they aren't saying much." He left the area, closing the door behind him.

"Are you alright?"

Amanda and Jennifer both nodded. Maria didn't move.

"You need to tell Sheriff Malone the truth. I know you didn't kill Silvia," I said, looking pointedly at Amanda.

"What makes you say that?" she asked through clenched teeth.

"I saw your face when the sheriff said the knife was in your room. You were as surprised as anyone."

Amanda sighed, and Jennifer burst into more tears. She looked like she'd probably spent all night crying.

"So what's your theory?" Amanda asked.

I shrugged. "Just a guess. I have no evidence. I think Jennifer drugged Silvia. Silvia didn't go to sleep. She went into the hall. Eric stabbed her and threw her down the stairs."

Maria sat up and stared at me. "You don't think Kyle did it?"

"I think Kyle is a horrible person, but not the killer."

Maria's forehead furrowed, and she picked at her fingernail.

"Eric wouldn't do that," Jennifer said, wiping her eyes.

"Even if he didn't, he's no better than Kyle," I said.

"What do you mean?"

I rubbed my arm. I didn't feel comfortable telling them everything Eric had said. "He wasn't going to wait for you," I told Jennifer. "He told me. He's been using you."

She looked at her hands. "I think I've always known that, but I didn't want to believe it."

"Do you know anything that could be helpful?"

Jennifer shook her head. I looked at Amanda. She just sank down next to her sister.

Maria let out a long breath. "If Kyle didn't do it, I blew up the sheriff's truck for no reason."

"Why would you try to help someone cover a murder?" I asked. "Especially someone terrible to you?"

"Because I love him."

I resisted rolling my eyes. Maria wasn't going to be any help. She didn't know anything.

"Why would Eric kill Silvia?" Jennifer asked.

"My guess? He knew there was another will, and he wanted to be done with her. If he could marry you, he knew you would get a large inheritance. The only thing I can't figure out is Amanda. Why are you covering for him?"

"I don't know what you're talking about."

"Did you kill Silvia?"

"I'm not answering."

"I don't believe you did. I saw you share a look with Eric."

Amanda bit her lip and looked at the ceiling. "I hate Eric. He's been threatening me for years."

"What?" Jennifer asked. "Why didn't you tell me?"

"He scares me, alright? I knew the two of you were together. I never liked him. I told him I was going to tell Dad about the two of you. He said if I did, he would hurt you. A few nights ago, he came and told me things were changing forever. He told me if I messed with any of it, he would kill both of us."

Jennifer gasped.

Amanda took a deep breath. "When the sheriff found the knife, Eric looked at me, and I knew. That's what he didn't want me to tell. I'd rather be in jail than dead."

"I wish you would have told me clear at the beginning," Jennifer said, wiping her eyes.

"He scared me." The sisters hugged each other.

"I think the wrong people are in here," Maria said.

I shrugged. "You still blew up a truck and ruined evidence, and Jennifer was drugging her aunt."

Maria sighed and lay back down.

"I'll bring you all some cookies later." I opened the door and almost knocked it into Jett. He followed me past Ledford and into the frigid Kansas air. We stood on the sidewalk, looking at the snow-covered world. "You were eavesdropping."

He grinned and held up a device. "And recording it. I'm not sure how well it worked, though."

"Did anyone find Eric?"

"Nope. Just your car. It was out of gas on the side of the road. Eric's footprints weren't anywhere near the car, so we have no idea. Someone must have picked him up on the side of the road."

"How could he not leave prints?"

"He probably just stepped on the plowed road. The ice that's left is too hard for someone to make prints in."

I breathed out and watched my icy breath.

"Do you think I'm right about him killing Silvia now?"

He stuck his hands in his coat pockets. "Probably. I'm just confused. If everyone knew there was a real will somewhere, getting that into the open would give everyone more money than they would ever need. Why kill Silvia?"

"Maybe they didn't kill her only because of the will. No one seemed to like her. Did the forensics find anything?"

"No. The knife was taken in to check for prints, but I haven't heard back."

"Now I have a car with no gas and no key," I said.

"Where's the key?" Jett asked.

I felt my face get warm. "I thought the car would stop if I threw it out the window. It didn't."

Jett laughed. "We could go look for it, but I'm not sure how good our chances are. I'll pick up some gas for you, but I think you'll have to go to a dealership for a key. Those keys are expensive."

"I had the key in my pocket," I said, putting my hand in the pocket. "That's how Eric was able to take the car." I pulled a paper from my pocket and unfolded it.

"What is it?" Jett asked, leaning over.

My eyes widened. "Zeb Clements's will."

Chapter 18

The muffins I'd just pulled from the oven were flat. I put them on the island and blew out a breath. We hadn't had many customers anyway. The roads were clear enough that the contractors working on my expansion had come. I could hear the hammering overhead. They had finished making the diner larger, and now they were working on expanding my living space.

I couldn't stop thinking about the will. Why had Eric put it in my coat pocket? We didn't need the will. We had the picture I'd taken. Eric made little sense to me, but maybe I should be happy not to understand the mind of someone like him.

Trina, one of the servers, came in. "Deputy Ledford is here, and he ordered food."

José turned from the stove. "Like a meal, not just dessert?"

"Yep. He ordered a burger."

Carrie nodded and went to the freezer.

"I bet he's going to try to get out of paying at the end," José said.

I had the same thought, but I would give him the benefit of the doubt. I waited until his food was cooked so I could take it to him. He wasn't always nice to the servers, and I didn't want him bothering Trina.

I took it out and placed it in front of him with a fake smile. "I hope you enjoy it."

"Why don't you sit and talk to me while I eat?" he asked.

I tried not to sigh as I sat. There was nothing he might say that could make my day more pleasant.

Ledford grabbed the ketchup and squirted it all over his fries. He shoved one in his mouth. "You know you're hurting Sheriff Malone's image, don't you? I'm having a hard time understanding why you would do that." He looked intently at me while he chewed.

"His image is fine. I think you're imagining things."

"People are beginning to talk. It's not good for public figures when gossip starts."

I pushed my hair behind my ear and leaned my elbows on the table. "What are they saying?"

"That you're distracting him from his work."

"People are saying this, or you are saying this?"

"The mayor of Muddy Creek isn't happy about it."

"That's because of what you told him, so if anyone is hurting his image, it's you."

His eyes narrowed. "I've heard he was a good sheriff before you came to town."

I gritted my teeth. "He's an excellent sheriff."

He laughed with no humor. "Says you."

The door opened, and Jett walked in. He frowned when he spotted me talking to Ledford.

"It's a shame, really," Ledford said.

"Your dinner is on the house," I said.

"It's about time."

I'm sure I wouldn't have done it if I'd taken two seconds to think, but I didn't. I grabbed his plate and dumped it upside down on his lap. He sputtered something, and I turned and ran out of the dining area to the stairs and up to my room. I didn't look to see Jett's expression.

I slammed the door and locked it. I hadn't done something like that since—since ever. I sat on my bed and covered my face with my hands. They were shaking, and I told myself not to cry. I'm not a crier, but it had been a long week, and what if Ledford was right? I knew Jett was a good sheriff, but what if I hurt his image?

I couldn't believe I was falling apart over this. I'd been through a lot worse and kept my cool. A tear trickled down my face, and I angrily wiped it away. I probably didn't have to worry about it anyway. Jett had pretty much said that part of our relationship was over. More tears rolled down my cheeks. That was why I was upset. It wasn't what Ledford said. I was in love with Jett, and I didn't know how to deal with it.

"Ivy?" Jett said through the door. He knocked. "Ivy? Let me in."

I grabbed a tissue from my nightstand and blew my nose.

He rattled the doorknob. "Ivy, come on. Let me in."

"Go away," I said. He was the last person I wanted to fall apart on. I couldn't tell him I was crying because I was tired and I wanted him to love me.

"Open the door."

"No."

It was quiet for a minute, then I saw the lock turn. I frowned as the door slowly opened, and Jett poked his head in. His mouth turned down.

"How did you unlock the door?" I asked, wiping my eyes.

He came in and shut the door. He held up a key.

"Where did you get a key?"

"I changed your locks, remember?"

"And you kept the spare?"

He smiled slightly. "I knew you'd lock me out someday."

"You can't do that. It's illegal."

He came and sat next to me on the bed. "Probably."

I held out my hand. "Give me the key."

He grinned as he dropped it in his shirt pocket. I didn't really care that he had the key, but arguing over that was better than talking about other things.

His expression became serious. "What did Ledford say?"

"It doesn't matter."

"You're crying."

I shook my head. "I'm tired."

"Why won't you tell me what he said?"

"It wasn't anything."

"You dumped his food on his lap."

"I hope it ruined his pants."

"See? Something's wrong. That doesn't sound like you."

"He's just rude. I wish he wouldn't come in here."

"I threw him out."

My eyes widened. "What?"

"He's the second person I've thrown out a door this week for you." He smiled and placed his hand on my cheek. "What are you doing to me?"

"Are you going to get in trouble?"

"I doubt it. Who is he going to complain to? I don't know what he said to you, but you don't usually dump a person's food on their lap." He put his arm around me, and I leaned against him.

Creepers jumped on the bed and curled up against Jett. Jett patted him on the back. I had a feeling Jett hadn't been around a lot of cats. He always seemed a little awkward when he petted him.

He sat there for a minute. I knew Jett wanted me to talk, but I couldn't. It was too awkward.

"Boyd called me," he finally said. "He wants to buy me a new truck. He said it would be a tax write-off."

"That's nice." We sat for a few more uncomfortable moments.

He sighed. "What did Ledford say?"

"Can't we talk about the truck?"

"No."

I sighed. "It wasn't really anything. He's just been making me angry for so long I finally lost it."

"If it wasn't really anything, tell me."

"He said I'm hurting your image."

"That's not true. He's just got some weird ideas. He thinks I should have no personal life. Plenty of sheriffs date or are married, and you don't see their deputies throwing tantrums. It's probably because he has no personal life. He wants everyone to be miserable like him."

I looked up at him. "I don't want to hurt your image."

He kissed the tip of my nose. "You never would. You're a respected member of the town. If anything, you make me look better."

I wondered how to interpret that. He didn't sound like he was going to distance himself from me. His eyes were studying mine. My stomach started to turn, which meant

I was either waiting for him to kiss me or deciding whether I should kiss him. But what if he really didn't want that part of our relationship? I didn't want to push it.

Standing, I walked to the window. "I'm sorry I overreacted down there. I don't think I can apologize to Ledford."

"He brought it on himself." He stood and came up behind me and put his arms around me. I put my hands on his, and we stood there staring at the lightly falling snow. He rubbed his cheek against mine, and I closed my eyes.

Someone knocked on the door, and I jumped. "Who is it?"

"José."

"Is everything alright?" I asked.

"That's what I wanted to know. Trina said Jett threw Ledford out of the diner and that you were upset."

"I'm fine."

Jett opened his mouth to talk, and I covered it with my hand. I'd probably already stirred up enough gossip for one day. Jett grinned.

"I'll text you when it's safe for you to come down," I whispered. I didn't want anyone to see him coming down. I opened the door and quickly slipped out, shutting it behind me.

"Have you been crying?" José asked.

"Is it that obvious?"

"No. Your eyes are just a little puffy, and I assumed you were upset from what Trina said."

"Can we ban Ledford? I don't know what that guy's problem is."

"That might cause other problems."

I walked down the stairs and turned my head slightly so the one table of customers wouldn't see my face. We walked into the kitchen, and I turned.

"Wait, why did I come down?" I asked. "Did you need me?"

"Nope. I was just checking on you. What happened to your cheek?"

I touched the spot where Jett had rubbed his face against mine, and I felt my face burn red. "Oh, I don't know."

"If I didn't know any better, I would think it was whisker burn." He walked over to the stove, and I glared at him.

I wasn't in the mood to bake, so I watched the dining area. It wasn't busy, but every time someone else was about to leave, another small group would come in.

Poor Jett had been stuck up there for a long time. The bell above the diner rang, and Jett walked in the front door. My eyes went wide.

José looked up. "He must have gone out the window."

"What?" I asked.

"What?"

I rolled my eyes and went to meet Jett. "Did you go out the window?" I whispered.

He nodded. "And it wasn't easy. That's a big drop."

"What if someone saw you?"

He patted me on the head and went into the kitchen.

"Hey, Jett," José said. "What have you been up to?"

"All sorts of stuff."

I wanted to throw something at José. I should just be happy Boyd wasn't here to tease me as well.

"Did you see Ivy's cheek?" José asked.

I turned away and wanted to scream. Who was the boss around here, anyway?

"What happened to your cheek?" he asked.

"Nothing," I said.

"It's almost as if someone with two to five days worth of stubble rubbed their cheek against hers."

"Oh my heck, José!" I said. "Do you want to be fired?"

He laughed, and so did Jett. Carrie looked at the two of them like they were crazy.

I grabbed the garbage bag and pulled it shut. "I'm taking out the garbage." I went out the back door and over to the dumpster. Boyd had been rubbing off on José, and I wasn't sure how I felt about that. It would be nice if José rubbed off on Boyd and not the other way around.

Chapter 19

My eyes popped open, and I stared at my dark ceiling. Someone was downstairs. It couldn't be morning. It was too dark for José to have come in. I reached past Creepers and grabbed my phone from the nightstand. 12:15 a.m. Definitely not José. Whoever was down there wasn't trying to be quiet. It sounded like they were moving pots and pans. Maybe throwing them onto the table.

If this was a robbery, it was probably best to stay up here. I grabbed Creepers and pulled him onto my lap. There was a chance the person doing it didn't know I lived here. Plenty of people knew I lived here, but I didn't advertise it. With luck, they would take the money in the cash register and leave.

I wondered for a moment if it might be Jett. He had changed all my locks, so he might have a key to the diner. I shook my head. He would have no reason to go rummaging around in the middle of the night.

I thought about calling 911, but they would call Jett. I might as well skip that step. My hand shook as I scrolled to his number and pushed the call button. It rang four times before he answered.

"Hey," he said groggily.

"There's someone in the diner," I said quietly.

"Are you sure?"

"Yes. I can hear them down there."

"On my way. Get in the closet." He hung up.

I sighed. I didn't want to get in the closet. If someone came up here, that was the first place they would look. There wasn't anywhere else to hide. The construction workers were building a living room on the other side of my room, but they hadn't connected the areas yet. I thought about going out the window, but I wasn't as daring as Jett.

I sucked in a breath. Someone was coming up the stairs. I got out of bed and put Creepers in the bathroom. I grabbed my pepper spray and flipped it open. The doorknob turned, and I held my breath.

"Ivy?" Eric said on the other side of the door. I didn't answer. "Ivy, I know you're in there."

My heart beat louder than it should have been possible, and I was sure everyone in town could hear it.

Eric slammed into the door, and I heard him swear on the other side. I was terrified, but I almost laughed. Jett had replaced all my doors when he was securing the place, and they were solid.

"Open the door, Ivy!" he yelled.

"The police are on their way," I said. "They should be here any second!"

He laughed. "You mean Sheriff Malone? I'm not worried about him."

"You should be. He tossed you out of the kitchen pretty easily the other day."

"Give me the will, and I'll be gone."

"Why?"

"Why do you care? Just give it to me."

I moved closer to the door now that I knew it was as strong as it was. "The will won't help you. It's not a secret. Why did you put it in my coat?"

"I had it on me since it came in the mail. I put it in your coat in case someone searched me, but then I had the idea to take you and leave. You should have stayed. We could have made an awesome couple."

"You're delusional."

"Right. You have your sheriff."

I swallowed. Jett better hurry.

I heard a crash downstairs, and I jumped.

"That's the sheriff now, I bet. I'm sure my friend is dealing with him."

I rubbed my lips together. This wasn't good. I didn't even have the will. Jett had taken it.

"Jennifer isn't going to give you anything no matter what the will says. She knows you're no good. Everyone does. Getting the will won't benefit you in any way."

"That's what you think. I don't need Jennifer anymore. Just open the door, and we can talk."

"We're talking now." I wasn't sure what to do. Noises from downstairs were making me nervous.

"I have a way to get a lot of money. Come with me, and I'll give you some. We can disappear to an island somewhere. "

"How much is a lot?" I asked, trying to think.

"Half a million."

I was quiet for a moment. What was Eric's game? How did he think he would get the money?

"I'm not leaving my diner for half a million. I could get more than that if I sold it." I had to let him think I was bribeable and not just trying to trick him.

"Fine. A million."

"How much are you getting?"

He sighed. "Does it really matter?"

"Yes."

"I'll get ten million."

"Then I want three million." I felt stupid saying it, but I felt Eric was even stupider for believing I would leave with him.

"Fine."

I unlocked the door slowly, and Eric pushed his way in.

"Where's the will?" he asked.

"Downstairs. I don't understand how the will give you money. I read it, and it had nothing in it about you."

"It doesn't give me money. It gives Kyle money, and he will give me money."

"Why? Kyle doesn't need you to get the money."

Eric smiled. "But Kyle doesn't know that. He's never seen the will. I told him Jett lied and most of it would go to his uncle, but that I could change it."

"And he believed you?"

"Of course. We've been friends for years." He put his arms around my waist, and I forced myself not to cringe. "I knew you would come around. Everyone has their price."

I grinned. "It's a good thing you're attractive, or I would have asked for five million."

He laughed and leaned toward me. How could he possibly believe I'd switched sides so easily? Maybe corrupt people think everyone is corrupt. He kissed me. He actually kissed me. It was fast, but I felt like I needed to wash my lips.

"Come on," he said.

He started down the stairs, and I took a deep breath. I didn't know what was happening downstairs with Jett, and I worried this was my only chance, so I kicked with everything in me. My foot made contact with Eric's back, and he fell down the hard wooden stairs, yelling as he fell. I ran down after him, not allowing him time to recover.

I jumped over him and ran to the dining area. Jett was handcuffing Kyle to a chair. Kyle's eye was swollen, his lip was bleeding, and Deputy Ledford was holding a gun on him. Jett must have called him. I'd worried for no reason.

"What was that crash?" Jett asked.

"I kicked Eric down the stairs."

Ledford rushed over to where Eric was trying to get to his feet. His head was bleeding, and he wobbled. Ledford grabbed him before he could gather his wits and handcuffed him.

"The jail isn't big enough for this," Ledford said, pushing Eric forward. Ledford looked small standing next to Eric, but he looked fierce.

"This is all Eric's fault," Kyle said. "He's behind all of it."

"Traitor," Eric said. "We wouldn't be in this situation if you were better at your job!"

"You told me to expect the sheriff. You didn't say he would have someone with him! And what about you? You let a woman kick you down the stairs!"

Eric glared at me. "You could have killed me."

"Like you killed Silvia?"

"She deserved it. No one disagrees. She stole from her own family. If she had just let the original will play out, all of her family would have had the money, and it wouldn't have had to go like this."

"You aren't her family, so it wouldn't have gone to you anyway," Jett said.

"But it would have gone to Jennifer," I said. "He's been in this for the long game."

"All of you walk," Jett commanded. "Ivy, follow, I don't want you here alone."

"I'm in my pajamas," I protested.

"I'll give you two minutes."

I rolled my eyes and ran upstairs. I pulled on my boots and grabbed my coat. I didn't feel like getting dressed in the middle of the night. Creepers meowed from the bathroom, so I opened the door, and he jumped on my bed.

I hurried down the stairs and followed Jett and Ledford, and they held guns to the prisoners. We walked to the jail, and Ledford kept the gun pointed at them while Jett moved Maria to the cell with Amanda and Jennifer.

The women were all surprised from being woken in the night, and none of them looked pleased to see their new prison mates. Kyle sank into one of the beds. Eric stood glaring at everyone.

"Do we get another bed?" Maria asked.

"No," Jett said. He unlocked the cell again. "Amanda can leave." Amanda looked from Jett to Jennifer.

"Go," Jennifer said. "I'll be fine."

Amanda nodded and left the cell.

"Ledford, go get Amanda a room at the bed-and-break-fast."

Ledford nodded. "It's a little late."

"Amanda, I want you to stay there for a few days until we can double-check some things."

"Alright. Can I call my dad?"

"I'll give you your cell phone back." They left the area and closed the door. Jett opened his desk and pulled out a phone and handed it to Amanda. He also handed her a coat that must be hers. She pulled it on and followed Ledford out the door. Jett and I were right behind.

"I'm going to take Ivy home," Jett said.

Ledford kept moving forward. "Of course you will."

"I need to make sure the diner is secure." We walked in silence. I rubbed my lips. I wasn't sure why that lame kiss bugged me so much. I unlocked the door, and Jett went around the diner, looking at all the windows.

I hurried upstairs and checked on Creepers. He was asleep on my pillow. I went back down into the kitchen. It was a mess.

"When Kyle saw us, he started throwing pans," Jett said, picking one up and putting it on the counter. "It looks like they came through the kitchen window. It's not broken."

"Did you punch Kyle?" I asked, picking up a pot.

"Yep, and I managed to get through this entire thing without getting a black eye of my own."

I smiled. "That is a miracle. Eric's head was bleeding."

"Right." Jett pulled out his phone and sent a text. "I told Ledford to go give him a rag or something. It didn't look too bad."

I picked up two more pots and sighed.

"What's wrong?"

"Nothing."

Jett tilted his head. "The nothing that means nothing? Or the nothing that means something?"

My mouth turned down. I really had trouble hiding my emotions. "I'm not sure I want to talk about it. Especially to you."

He frowned and took my hand. I couldn't wait until my living quarters were expanded, and I actually had a sitting room. He led me to a booth, and we sat across from each other.

I stared down at my hands. "When you do your police work, how do you know if you're going too far?"

He reached across and took my hand. "It's hard sometimes. Especially when you can't plan for what happens."

I bit the side of my cheek. I hoped this wasn't the end of whatever was happening with us, but if I didn't say it, I was sure Eric would, eventually. "Eric kissed me, and now I feel sick."

He released my hand and leaned back against the seat.

"I was scared and wanted him to think I agreed to his stupid plan. It only lasted a second, but it will bother me forever." My heart pounded as I wondered what Jett was thinking.

Jett stood and came to my side. He took my hand and pulled me to my feet. "Don't let a second ruin your sleep."

"I'm not sure I'll be able to help it," I admitted.

"Then let me give you something better to dream about." Eric's kiss fled from my mind when Jett's mouth found mine. I wrapped my arms around his neck. My heart felt warm, and I was sure I wanted to spend the rest of my life only kissing Jett. I could only hope he felt the same.

Chapter 20

"Is this how you ease us in?" Opal complained as one song ended and another started.

Opal was always a complainer, so I just smiled and kept dancing. I'd started my Zumba class again. Telling myself it took too much time wasn't actually true. I taught it early in the morning, and exercising was more beneficial than inconvenient.

"If I can do this, you can do this, Opal!" Boyd said, throwing his hands in the air.

I smiled as I watched Boyd. He didn't do any of the moves right, but he was enthused. His short shorts and knee-high socks would make anyone stop and smile. He had a neon blue sweatband on his head, and his goatee was coming in nicely. I had a room full of fifteen women and Boyd.

I'd slacked on my workouts, and I was feeling it. I would probably be stiff tomorrow, but it felt great at the same time.

Barbra was moving pretty well for a person in her seventies. Her purple ponytail flew through the air with each move. Most of the others were barely picking up their feet, but they would get better.

I'd rented the studio from a man in town. It was a little run down, but it still had nice big mirrors, and the floor was in good shape. I was glad the mirrors were behind me because I didn't want to see myself jumping around.

The door opened, and Jett came in. He wore his tan sheriff shirt and badge. Leaning against the wall, he crossed his arms and smiled. It was an interesting thing to watch. Not a person in my class was under fifty, and they all had determined looks. Well, all except Opal. She was just there for the social aspect.

The song ended, and I pointed at Jett. "Hey, ladies. Oh and Boyd. It looks like the sheriff will join us today."

Everyone turned, and Jett frowned. "No, no, no. I'm just here to watch."

Barbra put her hands to her waist. "There is no coming to watch. You participate, or you can leave."

He chuckled. "I'm not dressed for it."

Barbra glared. "Look at us. Most of us are wearing whatever we found lying around the house. You're fine."

I giggled. Barbra was wearing a pink leotard with leopard print leggings. She was right. The style in this room was anything goes.

"Come on, Sheriff," I said. "Are you afraid we'll outdance you?"

"I'm sure of it."

"If I can do it, you can," Boyd said.

I winked. "It's our first time back. None of us are great at it."

"Sheriff, Sheriff, Sheriff!" Barbra began chanting. The room all picked up the chant, and Jett sighed and nodded.

I began dancing again, and I had to turn away from Jett so I wouldn't burst into laughter. Each move he did was stiff, and he looked like he might make a run for it. I had planned to stop after this song, but I did one extra just for Jett's benefit.

When the class ended, it took everyone twenty minutes to clear out. I'd finally told them all they could go get a free dessert at the diner so they would leave.

Jett and I were the last to go. I grabbed my things and turned to him. "You should come more often. It's good for you."

He shook his head. "That was awful. My body doesn't want to move like that. I prefer weights."

"The more you do it, the easier it is."

"I'm sure. I didn't actually come to dance."

"Really?" I teased.

"I came to show you my new wheels."

"You replaced your truck?"

He grinned. "Boyd took me into Wichita and bought it for me. We even took it in and had all the police sirens and stuff installed. It's awesome, come on." He grabbed my hand and pulled me out the door.

"Whoa," I said, when I saw the—vehicle sitting on the side of the street. "That's... interesting." I didn't have any other words. It looked like a futuristic blow-up toy with its sharp angles and metal finish. "It's a truck?"

"It's a Tesla Cybertruck."

"Okay." It said *County Sheriff* on the side.

"Get in. I'll take you to the diner."

The diner was only a two-minute walk, but I would let Jett show off his odd truck. I climbed in. It was spacious and had the new-car smell.

Jett got in and grinned. "Watch." Blue and red lights flashed in the windows, and a siren went off. I cringed and resisted covering my ears. "You have your judgy face on. It's because your friend Elon is behind it, isn't it?"

"No, it's great. Just a little weird. People will definitely know it's you coming."

"I know, right? I can't believe Boyd bought it just like it was nothing. And the best thing? It belongs to me, not the county. I had to get permission and have it inspected."

"I didn't know Boyd had that kind of money."

"He doesn't flaunt it, obviously, but he sold his farm-land for a pretty nice deal. He's a millionaire."

"What? That doesn't seem possible." I thought about Boyd and all his behaviors, and none of them marked him as wealthy.

"He said he wasn't letting money change him, so he doesn't use much of it. I wanted you to be the first to see it. I did have to stop and talk to Lionel, but then I came straight here."

"How is Lionel?" It had been three weeks since Eric and Kyle had been arrested.

"Good. He's moving to California with Amanda after all the trials are over. Now, are you ready?" He put on his dark sunglasses and smiled at me.

I grinned. "Of course I'm ready."

Jett pulled away from the curb, and we drove down the street.

"It feels so big inside."

"It's definitely a beast. I'll drive you all over town before I take you to the diner."

"How do you think all the trials will go?" I asked.

"I'm pretty sure they'll be fairly straightforward. Maria and Jennifer are taking responsibility for their parts. Kyle will be charged with breaking and entering and assaulting an officer. It doesn't seem like he had anything to do with the murder. Eric denied everything, but his prints were on Amanda's bookcase and the false book. He claimed he was never in there. His prints were also all over the closet we found Silvia's body in."

"Will I have to testify?"

"Yep. Probably in all the cases. Sorry about that."

"It's fine. How can you drive this thing? It's massive."

He grinned and pointed at the back. "And it can fit three car seats comfortably."

My heart stopped. "And you're planning on putting three car seats back there?"

He shrugged. "It doesn't hurt to be prepared."

A separator had been placed behind the front seat to separate Jett from any criminals. I was pretty sure it wasn't to protect him from babies throwing things.

"So you're arresting kids now?"

He chuckled. "Since the truck is mine, I can use it when I'm off duty. If that ever happens, anyway."

I did what I knew how to do best. Changed the subject. "You've had a crazy month. Do you get a break?"

"Nope. Some college kids are setting up some sort of camp just outside town. I'm sure it's harmless, but the mayor's uptight about it. He wants me to go make sure they aren't building or doing anything that goes against any laws."

"Does the mayor usually tell you what to do?"

"No. For the most part, he doesn't do much of anything, but he's been bothering me a lot since the Clementses' case. I think it annoyed him not to be the one calling all the shots, so now he's trying to make me look incompetent. He's also a big Ledford supporter. If he runs against me in the next election, the mayor will back him for sure."

"He still won't win. Everyone loves you."

He grinned and looked over his sunglasses. "Everyone, huh?"

I smiled. "Everyone."

Watch for *Murder With a Drizzle of Syrup*.

Cinnamon Rolls
2 Tbsp yeast
1 Tbsp sugar
½ c. water
1 c. water
1 c. scalded milk
6 Tbsp butter
1 c. sugar
3 eggs
7 c. flour
1 tsp salt
Cinnamon
Sugar

Activate the Yeast: In a small bowl, dissolve the yeast in warm water. Set aside until it becomes frothy.

Prepare the Wet Ingredients: Scald the milk, then combine it with the water, melted butter, sugar, and eggs in a large mixing bowl. Beat the mixture until smooth and well-blended.

Incorporate the Yeast: Add the activated yeast to the wet ingredients and mix thoroughly.

Combine with Dry Ingredients: Gradually add the dry ingredients to the wet mixture, kneading until a smooth dough forms.

First Rise: Cover the bowl with a clean kitchen towel or plastic wrap. Let the dough rise in a warm place until it doubles in size, about 1-2 hours.

Second Rise: Once the dough has risen, punch it down to release air bubbles. Cover again and let it rise for another 30 minutes.

Prepare the Dough: Turn the dough out onto a floured surface and knead briefly. Roll it out into a rectangle.

Add Filling: Spread a thin, even layer of butter over the surface of the dough. Generously sprinkle with cinnamon and sugar.

Shape and Slice: Roll the dough tightly into a log, starting from one long edge. Pinch the seam to seal. Slice the roll into 1-inch thick pieces.

Prepare for Baking: Arrange the slices on a greased baking sheet, leaving space for them to expand.

Bake: Preheat your oven to 325°F (165°C). Bake the rolls for 20 minutes or until golden brown.

Cool and Serve: Let the cinnamon rolls cool slightly before serving. Enjoy warm!

Also By Kristy Dixon

<u>Cozy Mystery</u>
Murder With a Side of Bacon
Murder With a Hint of Cinnamon
Murder With a Fudge Brownie to Go

<u>Young Adult</u>
Akkron (The Silver Eclipse Book 1)
Boztoll (The Silver Eclipse Book 2)
The Other Continent (The Silver Eclipse Book 3)
The Amethyst Crown
More Than Once Upon a Time

Trapped In Once Upon a Timen
The Beginning of Once Upon a Time

<u>**Coming Soon!**</u>
Mermaid's Demise (Riviand Lost Book 2)
Dragon's Cove (Riviand Lost Book 3)
Murder With a Splash of Vanilla
Murder With a Drizzle of Syrup

About the Author

Kristy Dixon started writing stories when she was seven and never stopped. She enjoys writing cozy mysteries and YA. At home, she spends her time playing board games with her husband and kids and writing. Occasionally she takes part in a Super Mario marathon. She has six chickens and a cat that help keep life amusing. If she isn't playing with her kids or writing, she is usually eating cookies, or wishing she was eating cookies.